Samuel Cox

Miracles; an argument and a challenge

Samuel Cox

Miracles; an argument and a challenge

ISBN/EAN: 9783741192746

Manufactured in Europe, USA, Canada, Australia, Japa

Cover: Foto ©Andreas Hilbeck / pixelio.de

Manufactured and distributed by brebook publishing software
(www.brebook.com)

Samuel Cox

Miracles; an argument and a challenge

PREFACE.

———◦◦———

THE following essay is composed of three Articles which appeared in *The Expositor* for A.D. 1882 and 1883. In its earlier form it attracted an unusual share of attention, and I have been much pressed to reprint it in a separate and more convenient form, both by many young men who profess to have derived benefit from it, and who therefore wish to put it into the hands of certain of their comrades, and by many ministers and clergymen who love young men, and long to save them from drifting into a cold and barren scepticism. As a rule, publishers do not look on small books with favourable eyes. But at last I am able to comply with the request by which I have been honoured. And it will be a very great reward for any trouble I have been at, if I should find that the argument here offered to them has proved an " aid to faith " to any of the class to which it is specially addressed.

In writing it out I made no attempt to be original. I endeavoured rather to gather up in a compact and handy form the argument in favour of *Miracles* which now commends itself to the more thoughtful and intelligent advocates of the Christian Faith. I drew my materials, as I have confessed, mainly from a chapter in Newman Smyth's *Old Faiths in New Light*, from one of Godet's *Lectures in Defence of the Christian Faith*, and from an essay of my own on *Prayer*, which appeared in *The Expositor* for A.D. 1877. I was also indebted for valuable suggestions to my friends T. T. Lynch and Dr. Wace. The germs of my argument are also, as I have since ascertained, to be found in the writings of

Horace Bushnell and Edward Irving. Indeed, I doubt whether they are absent from the works of any considerable member of the broader school of theology, from the time of Coleridge down to the present day. And, finally, this argument has been woven into a treatise of extraordinary force by William Arthur, M.A., which has appeared since these Articles were published. It is called the Fernley Lecture for 1883 (London: T. Woolmer); its theme is *The Difference between Physical and Moral Law,* and in developing his theme, Mr. Arthur meets, and in my judgment triumphantly refutes, the sceptical or infidel arguments of Comte, Herbert Spencer, John Stuart Mill, and George Henry Lewes. If young men, "perplext by doubt," will but study this elaborate and masterly treatise as carefully as it deserves, they will soon "beat their music out."

I lay stress on the non-originality of the substance of my main line of argument for two reasons. (1) I want my readers to feel that they are not listening to a single voice, but to the blended and consenting voices of many of the men to whom the Church and the world owe most, and that, therefore, the argument here presented, however imperfectly, is really worthy of their best consideration.

And (2) I want, if I can, to provoke a response to the challenge with which my essay concludes from some candid and able opponent of the Christian Faith. I have read, I think, nearly all that the leading sceptics and agnostics have said on the subject of Miracles, but I have never fallen in with any reply to the argument contained in the last chapter of this book. And it is high time that such a reply, if reply is to be had, were forthcoming. For this argument is not mine, nor is it new. It is at least fifty years old, and it has satisfied men as sincere and as able as any of those who reject the conclusion to which it conducts. There are many of us who are eager to hear what can be said on the other side, who would listen to a counter-argument with candour and respect, and who, if fairly convinced of its superior force, would frankly acknowledge our defeat. We crave the truth, and truth in forms which the reason can grasp and defend. We believe that we hold the truth, and that we offer it to others on reasonable grounds. And so far from fearing any candid and sincere opposition, we respectfully invite the friends of reason and truth to drive us from the ground on which we stand, if they can. Will any of them take up the challenge? Let them reply to our argument either as it is briefly unfolded in this brief essay, or, better still, as it is philosophically and polemically elaborated in Mr. Arthur's most valuable treatise.

S. COX.

Nottingham.

CONTENTS.

MIRACLES.

CHAPTER I.

THE ORIGINAL MIRACLE.

IT is curious and a little pitiful to note how
Design and Evolution are pitted against each
other—as if the one were contrary to the other
—in much of the controversial literature of the
day, and how this illogical conflict on a false
issue culminates, just where it should find no
place, at the annual meetings of the British
Association. For, surely, it is not only obvious
that evolution may be simply a method in which
the creative design is worked out, but also that,
if it be, it implies a design far more subtle

B

profound, and far-reaching than that involved
in the older hypothesis of successive acts of
creation. If the whole infinitely varied round
of nature has been *pro-duced* from a single
point, if, so to speak, the whole universe has
grown from a single seed, He who created that
seed—assuming for a moment that it had a
Creator—and stored up in it the potencies
which it has unfolded and is to unfold through
incalculable æons, must have possessed a wisdom which we can hardly distinguish from
Omniscience, and a power which we can hardly
distinguish from Omnipotence; and all the
marks of design which we trace in the unfolded
flower must speak to us of a forethought more,
and not less, wonderful and divine than if that
flower had been built up petal by petal and
touched in tint by tint.

(2) Whether or not Evolution be the most
fitting and adequate word to describe, for the
present, the genesis of the universe, there can

be no doubt that a vast process of development
has taken place ; for all the sciences—*e.g.* astro-
nomy, geology, embryology—point to it with
one consent, and all the results of observation
and experience as they are read off by the most
competent interpreters. And yet, on consideration, even the most advanced and sceptical
philosopher must admit that Evolution is not
and cannot be the *final* word of science, though
it be the last it has yet uttered. For it does
not cover and explain all the facts of which
science takes cognizance, nor even the ultimate
and fundamental facts ; as, for example, the
origin of matter and force (if these be two, and
not one), the origin of life, the origin of consciousness. Great and marvellous as is the
advance which science has made during the last
fifty years, those who most triumphantly proclaim its advance, and are most competent to
appreciate it, will be the last to deny that it
has still greater victories to achieve in the future,

and that it is very far from having reached its goal. It will yet discover some higher law, speak some larger, nobler word—a word, perchance, which will cover and illuminate the fundamental problems which for the present it is compelled to leave unsolved, or even untouched. To pronounce Evolution the final word, to ban all who do not implicitly accept it as an adequate solution of the whole mystery of the universe, is therefore to sin, as against science herself, so also against that law of progress which has as surely governed all human discoveries as it has marked all the successions of nature. While, on the other hand, to deny development, to doubt that through the whole realm of nature there has been a slow, laborious, and gradual ascent from simple to more complex, from inferior to higher forms, is to be wilfully blind and deaf to the teaching of all the facts within our reach.

(3) It has been the constant misfortune of

Science to number among her votaries men who have so little of her spirit as to fulminate anathemas against all who do not accept her last as her final word, and adjust the whole circle of their beliefs to what may be only an unverifiable hypothesis, and is sure to prove an inadequate solution of the great problem. These bigots of science are as truly the worst enemies of science as the bigots of the church are the worst enemies of true religion. And he is the truly scientific man who rebukes and withstands these hasty and ignorant bigots in the name of science herself; and who, as he glances at the long muster roll of her triumphs, finds in it ample space for more and more glorious inscriptions than those which have already been so fairly written and so splendidly illuminated upon it. But even the bigots of science—no, nor even the hypocrites of science who, knowing more and better than her bigots, nevertheless stoop to support their narrow intolerant dogmas and to swell the volume of their anathemas—are not so untrue to their high calling and vocation as are those who, professing to believe in God as the Maker of all things and the Saviour of all men, nevertheless fear lest any accurate interpretation of his works should convict Him of having contradicted Himself, convict Him of being double-minded and double-voiced, so that, unless they "lie for Him," the "truth" cannot be known or cannot prevail. The perversion is so monstrous and unnatural that no severer condemnation of it is possible than the bare statement of it. Yet who can deny that there have been many "good men" who have thought to do God service by both misreading the Bible and refusing to read the book of science; *i.e.* by closing their eyes against the plain facts both of Scripture and of the natural universe?

(4) There is perhaps no one subject, there is surely no one document, which the bigots,

whether of science or of religion, have treated with more intolerable unfaithfulness and insin-cerity than the ancient tradition of the origin of all things which Moses has inserted in, with which he has commenced, the Book of Genesis. Yet, viewed fairly, looked at with the open eyes that desire the truth, with due consideration of its date, purpose, method, it may be doubted whether there is any one document over which true science and true religion could meet with heartier consent. Both have, and both should claim, an interest in it. The first chapter of the Bible is also the opening page of the book of science, and records her first veritable triumph ; nor, if only this first page be rightly read, has she done much more than confirm and expand it.

(5) How, then, may we reach or recover the right point of view ? In many ways, no doubt, if we only bring an honest and open mind to the task ; but none seems more valuable than

that suggested by the brief phrase (in Gen. i. 21), "And God created great whales;" for in these words we may find a key to the whole story of creation as narrated in the Book of Genesis. We approach this key as we observe that "great whales"—literally, "sea monsters," and doubtless alligators and crocodiles rather than whales would be in the author's mind—are the only creatures of whom specific mention is made in this Chapter, and consider the motive for mentioning them. It speaks indeed of domestic cattle and of wild beasts, but not of the lion or the ox; it speaks of the fowl of the air, and of the creeping things of the earth, but no one species of these genera is singled out for special note. It is only when we come to the fish of the sea, which the waters bring forth abundantly, that the creation of any single species is recorded, and a word is used which would call up in the minds of the first readers of this document an image of the monsters they had seen disporting themselves in the Nile. Now, why is that? No naturalist, no man of science, intent on purely scientific objects, would have written thus, or have made this solitary exception. No; and therefore in this exception we have a hint that the whole document was written not from a purely scientific or naturalistic but from a religious point of view. For the crocodile—regarded as a noble animal type, a fine symbol of Nature's work—was *worshipped* in Egypt. The Israelites had grown familiar with that worship in the house of their bondage, and were only too prone to revert to it, as their after history proves. By a single stroke of his pen, then, either Moses or the original author of the document, teaches them that the crocodile was not a god but a creature of God, and condemns the whole system of idolatry, of animal or nature worship, by which the world was then oppressed. Following up the phrase to its last resort, we find in it an attempt to free the minds of men from a more cruel bondage than that of Egypt, bondage to the mere brute forces of nature, and to raise them to their true place as lords of the natural world, and not its slaves.

(6) Nor is this the only hint contained in this Chapter of the religious intention by which it was inspired and shaped. It is full of such hints. Much easy satire has been expended, for example, on the Mosaic view of the function of sun, moon, and stars. According to Moses, we are told, the vast solar and sidereal systems have no other use than to give light to men, or to serve them "for signs and for seasons, and for days and for years." But, it is asked, can any rational mind believe that that vast array of bodies celestial was designed solely for the benefit of our tiny planet, or of the creatures who inhabit it?

Those who criticize Moses should at least, however, take the pains to place themselves

at his point of view. And as it is very obvious
that no reasonable and thoughtful man, writing
from the purely scientific or astronomical point
of view, could possibly imagine that sun, moon,
and stars were created solely for earthly uses,
and as moreover we have quite as good ground
for attributing the "godlike faculty" to this
great statesman and lawgiver as to any of his
critics, would it not be reasonable, as well as
charitable, to inquire both whether Moses does
affirm them to have no other use, and whether
in emphasizing this special use he may not have
had other than a scientific motive? In Chaldea,
the ancestral home of the sons of Abraham,
the great lights of heaven were worshipped as
themselves divine, and this lustrous celestial
veil was drawn over the face of the Almighty
and hid Him from his seeking children. May
not Moses then have written from a religious,
instead of a scientific, point of view? May he
not have made this emphatic and repeated

assertion of the creation of · sun, moon, and
stars, and of their ministry to man, in order
to withdraw the intercepting veil, in order to
teach us that we should worship none other
god than the Father of the lights, and to per-
suade us that even the glorious orbs of heaven,
to which men once paid divine honours, are
our servants and ministers, not our lords ?

If we but think ourselves back into the time
and place of Moses, remember that he was the
redeemer and mediator of Israel, that it was his
special mission to reveal God and his will to
them, and to lift them out of the ignorance and
bondage in which all races were then sunk ;
and then, with all this well in mind, turn to
his story of the creation, we shall find in it
a hundred proofs that it *was* written from the
religious, and not from the scientific, point of
view ; and that, in writing or in copying and
adapting it to his purpose, he was impelled by
the very motive which animated him throughout

his career ; viz. the desire to raise Israel, from its bondage to sense and nature, into the freedom and dignity proper to man and into the service and worship of the only true God.

(7) In insisting on this higher and religious motive, however, I do not for a moment admit that, even from a scientific point of view, much can be reasonably alleged against it, provided always that we read it with the same fairness which we are expected and bound to bring to the perusal of any scientific or sceptical treatise. It is a very ancient document that lies before us ; probably long anterior, in substance at least, to the time of Moses, though he may have recast it into its present shape. It is far and away the oldest document in the world. And we might fairly claim for it, therefore, that it should be read with the large allowance which is readily extended to almost every ancient document outside the covers of the Bible. It was primarily intended, moreover, for the instruction

of men to whom both science and letters were unknown. Hence it must of necessity be concise, simple, memorable, free from technical formulæ, couched in such plain terms as plain men use. The very utmost we could demand of it is that it should contain no demonstrable and fatal error; that it should be pliant to or leave room for the discoveries of widening science and experience; and that, to the end of time, it should fulfil some high moral or religious function. How happily it meets, how generously it outruns, these conditions has been demonstrated again and again, and is now very widely admitted, admitted the more frankly and heartily in proportion as its critics possess the erudition which enables them to compare it with the other ancient documents that cover, or profess to cover, the same ground. Those who possess even the slightest acquaintance with the cosmogonies and mythologies of ancient India, Egypt, Chaldea, Greece even, cannot but

confess that the story of the creation told by
Moses is simplicity and sobriety itself when
compared with *them;* that it is not bound up, as
they are, with monstrous and impossible mis-
readings both of the natural universe and of
the genesis of man ; and that its terms are so
simple, so general, so flexible as to leave verge
for any conclusions which science may reach.

The "days" of creation have, indeed, been
gravely denounced or lightly ridiculed from the
time when men began to let their reason play
freely on Scriptures which were long held to
be sacred from criticism. But many very competent critics now see in this "week of days"
only a mnemonic device which made it easier
to commit the story to memory and to hand
it down in an unbroken tradition ; while they
admit that the general order of creation, or of
evolution, given by Moses tallies, at least in its
main outlines, with the last hypotheses of science.
And of this we may be very sure, that if the

document recorded in the first chapter of Genesis had been discovered among the papyri of
Egypt or the inscriptions of Babylon, or even
if its substance had been traced in the discourses
of a Greek philosopher or the verses of a Latin
poet, the whole scientific and literary world,
even that small portion of it which girds at the
Bible, would have received it with an instant
chorus of admiration and astonishment ; while
if the " origins of things " which we find in
the sacred books of Asia, Africa, or Europe,
had been found between the covers of the Bible,
even the staunchest believer must have repu-
diated them, and, with them, the whole system
with which they were indissolubly intertwined.

(8) From the purely scientific point of view
the Mosaic account of the creation is no doubt
very defective, though it cannot fairly be said to
be inaccurate. But, as we have seen, it does not
profess to have been written from that point of
view ; and we need claim for it nothing more

than that it is the best conception of the genesis
of the universe which the world's "grey fathers"
were able to form or to receive. In such terms
as they could apprehend, the ancestral race of
man was taught that the world and all that it
contains came from God, that it was fashioned
by his wisdom, in a gradual orderly way, for a
definite and gracious end. It is philosophic
rather than scientific; *i.e.* it rather expresses
man's first and best thoughts concerning first
causes and their first effects than lays out in
order a scientific report of the origin of all
things. And why should we demand science
of Moses? No one expects to find in the Ten
Commandments a systematic code of laws, an
elaborate and complete scheme of jurisprudence.
Why, then, should we expect to find modern
science in the first chapter of Genesis any more
than we expect to find modern jurisprudence in
the Decalogue? All just legislation indeed
implies the fundamental moralities of the " Ten

C

Words " ; and so all science, truly so called,
implies the fundamental simplicities of the
opening document of Genesis. But to look
for a scientific treatise in Genesis is about as
wise as to look for an elaborate jurisprudence
in Exodus.

Nevertheless, when science has grown ripe, it
may be that its last, simplest, and grandest
generalizations will correspond, in a quite sur-
prising way, with the ancient and simple gene-
ralities of the Book of Genesis. And we may,
perhaps, find one hint of this correspondence in
the recent discoveries of the spectroscope. It
has been demonstrated that the very salts and
metals which we find in the earth exist in the
solar and sidereal light ; so that possibly light
may have in itself the constituent and origina-
tive germs of all terrestrial things, and, in the
most exact scientific sense, the universe may be
but a product, an incarnation and epiphany, of
light. But should that be so, will not this

generalization of science correspond very happily with the words of Moses, who tells us that, in his first creative fiat, God said, "Let there be light," creating first that from which, ex hypothesi, all else was to proceed?

Time was too, we may add in passing, when the existence of light, prior to the creation of sun, moon, and stars, was a theme for ridicule; but now that, in their study of the nebulæ, astronomers have discerned the existence of "a self-luminous substance, of an inconceivable tenuity, diffused over spaces so vast as to baffle every effort to define them," men of science proclaim as a fact that which they once ridiculed as absurd.

(9) But it is when we look at the Mosaic narrative as a whole that we see most clearly what room it leaves for the advancing discoveries of science, and how evidently it was cast into a portable and rememberable form. We are told at the outset that the earth was

"without form and void." It needed, therefore, first to be put into form, and then fitted or furnished. These two processes constituted the work of the six "days." These six days are divisible into two groups—a first three, and a second three. In the first three God gives form to the formless earth; in the second three He fills the void earth with an innumerable multitude of living things. That which is without form is without use; that which is void is not being used. God will not suffer the world to be either useless or unused. Only when it is drawn into shape and peopled with innumerable forms of life can He take delight in it. Hence God says of each day's work, "It is good"; but only when the end crowns the work, and the world is both formed and occupied, does He pronounce it "very good."

What are the steps or stages of this work? First, light springs up in darkness; second, the aerial heavens are divided from the waters;

third, the earth emerges from the deep, and
brings forth grass and herb; fourth, the great
lights are made to rule the day and to rule the
night; fifth, the fish of the sea and the fowl of
the air are called into being; sixth, the beasts
of the earth are formed, and man, the crown
and lord of them all. This is the work of the
six days; and these days, as I have said, may
be divided into two groups; a first three in
which God *forms* the formless earth, and a
second three in which He *fills* the empty
earth.

Look, then, at the first group, the formative
group. In these, we are told, God separates the
light from the darkness; then He separates the
aerial heaven from the heaving waters; and
then He separates the earth from the sea, and
causes it to bring forth and bud. Thus, by
successive acts of separation, the world is drawn
into form, drawn within bounds that define it;
the chaos is dissolved into its separate ele-

ments,* fire (light), air, water, earth. And these
four are evoked in the most philosophic order ;
i.e. from the finest and most subtle to the
grossest and coarsest. There is first the light,
which is the finest ; then there is the air, the
next in fineness ; then there is the water, which
is grosser, but still finer than the earth ; then
there is the earth itself, the grossest of them
all. Nay, more, these elemental acts of creation
culminate in vegetation, which embraces all
four of them. Its substance is of the earth
earthy ; its tissues are filled with water ; its
lungs breathe in and breathe out air ; and the
light, or heavenly fire, permeates its whole
being, giving it both its beauty and its fruit-
fulness.

And now let us take the second group of
days, and mark how exactly it corresponds to
the other ; how the fourth day answers to the

---

* Of course I use this word throughout in its popular, not in
its scientific sense.

first, the fifth to the second, the sixth to the
third. On the first day we have the genesis
of light out of darkness ; and on the fourth
day the sun, the lord of light, is made, as are
also those pure and sacred princes of darkness,
the moon and the stars. On the second day
the aerial firmament divides the upper from the
inferior waters ; and on the fifth the birds of
the air and the fish of the sea are created and
made. On the third day the solid earth is
formed ; and on the sixth day the earth brings
forth beast and cattle and creeping thing, each
after its kind. Nay, as the work of the first
three days, during which the elements were
created, culminated in vegetation which combines all the elements in itself, so the work
of the second three days, during which the
living creatures were called into being, culminated in man, who combines in himself all the
special faculties and virtues of the animate
world.

Obviously there is method here, there is design. And the design of the method is not only to help the memory and ensure an accurate tradition, but also to convey the thought that God put forth his creative powers according to a wise and divine order; first, creating the elements, from the finer and more subtle down to the grosser; and then furnishing the elements with animated forms of life, from the simpler and ruder to the more complex and perfect.

Men of science have laid so much stress on " the days " of this ancient narrative, that they have overlooked the wisdom and simplicity with which it conveys true and large impressions of the origin of all things. If, in a large simple way, speaking to the simple and unlettered on the genesis of the world, we were to speak thus: First, God gave shape to the shapeless earth, then He filled the empty earth; first He created the elements, beginning with the most subtle and creative, and coming down to

the most gross and material; then He filled
the elements with their appropriate tenants,
beginning now at the lowest end of the scale
and working upward from the most simple and
rudimentary structures to the most subtle, complex, perfect: if *that* were our story of the
creation, as it is that of Moses, would any
scientific man who believes in God the Maker
have much fault to find with it? Would he
not admit that, viewed as a large and simple
outline, it was true enough for all practical
purposes, and that it would be far more likely
to convey a fine moral impression to the popular
mind than a more detailed statement, such as
the science of to-day might put forth, only to
be corrected, if not contradicted, by the science
of a hundred, a thousand, or four or six
thousand, years hence? *

* In this ninth section I have been much indebted to some
imperfect notes I took of a most admirable and comprehensive
sermon preached by the late T. T. Lynch, some five and twenty
years since.

(10) The prime excellence of this Biblical
document is not, however, its simplicity, nor
its elasticity—giving scope to any discoveries
that science may make, nor even its general
accuracy when read historically and in a reasonable spirit ; but its religious inspiration and
motive. It sees, and teaches us to see, *God*
in all things. It puts Him behind and before
all things. And, moreover, it places all things
under *our* feet, so redeeming us from that fear
of the vast and irresistible forces of nature
which led unemancipated man to worship and
appease them, and teaching us to worship Him
only who is the Maker and Ruler of them all.
They are our ministers and subordinates, not
our lords; we have no Lord but Him. In
short, the Chapter contains the very charter
of science, as well as the fundamental truth
of religion. For so long as men *worshipped*
nature, they could not approach and study her
in a scientific spirit, any more than they could

worship Him who is a Spirit so long as He was veiled from them by the works of his hands.

Nor, in thus tracing all things to a spiritual origin, does Moses do more than science itself will warrant ; for science has no simpler hypothesis to offer us, nor any half so reasonable ; nay, by the lips of some of her most distinguished disciples, she frankly refuses to supply us with any hypothesis at all. Searching everywhere for the original cause of things, she is compelled to confess that she cannot find it in the things themselves ; that, while the method or order of physical sequences is familiar to her, their cause is unknown. The origin of matter, the origin of force, the origin of life, the origin of thought are all, by her own confession, beyond her reach. Even though she call Evolution to her aid, the problem is only pushed further back. It is not solved. It is no whit nearer to a solution. It has

to be handed over to reason and conscience
.after all.

And when we bend reason to the task of
judging the solution of this standing problem
which the Bible offers to our faith, reason con-
firms, and rejoices to confirm, the Biblical theory
of causation. For we ourselves, if we *have*
bodies, *are* spirits ; and therefore the conception
of a Spiritual Cause of all that we behold
cannot be alien to us. If it be, as it is, an
elementary axiom of science, that the effect can
contain nothing which was not in its cause, and
can never be greater than its cause, then, as
it is very certain that we find " spirit " in the
great effect which we call the universe—find
it at least in ourselves and in one another—
we are plainly entitled to infer that there must
be spirit in the Cause of this great effect.
We hold, and are warranted in holding, that
we must have derived our spirits from the
original and creative Spirit ; and that He must

be inconceivably greater than we are, since we and all things proceed from Him. Moreover, as we know that our spirits, our wills, rule and control our physical frame, and even pass out beyond our personal limits to affect and transform the face of the earth, we argue, not without some show of logic surely, that the great original Spirit must be able to rule and affect at his will the great and universal frame which sprang into being at his command.

(11) Even when we go away from and beyond ourselves, and watch the play and movement of the physical world, seeking to interpret it honestly and according to our best skill, we still meet with phenomena which speak to us of a Spirit behind it and working up through it ; in other words, we see nature herself straining up to God. For who can watch the face of nature, and study her history, without observing in every province of her domain the signs of an all-pervading intelligence, and struggles

by which she seeks to free herself from the
rigour of physical law, and to rise into a liberty
which is the proper attribute of spirit? Matter
itself is not purely materialistic, but is ever
lifting itself up toward the spiritual, as it could
hardly do were its Cause as material as itself.
If in its lower provinces, for example, it is
everywhere and absolutely subject to the law
of gravitation, yet even in that low stage in
which we come on the phenomena of crystalli-
zation, we observe a tendency to resent and shake
off that subjection and to rise into forms and
shape itself after an ideal impossible to it so
long as it maintains an undivided obedience
to this law; forms which by naming them
"ideal" we shew to have in them the suggestion of a Mind at work behind the material
atoms. Vegetable life marks another advance;
for here so many forces operate, and the result
is so complex, subtle, and wonderful, that
we cannot but feel that at this point we

enter on a much higher and freer mode of existence, and are brought into more immediate contact with a shaping and invisible Cause. Science may dissect the plant, name its parts, determine their functions; but it cannot create the tiniest moss that grows upon a rock, or tell us by what mystic forces it was created, or from whence those forces issued. In animal life we make yet another advance, a nearer approach to the intelligence, will, freedom, which are the proper attributes, not of matter, but of spirit. We reach the full diapason in man, finding in him a creature subject to natural laws and instincts indeed, but capable of controlling and modifying them in a thousand different ways; able to subdue the earth, to bend all other creatures to his will, to study and formulate the laws by which the universe is governed, to rule his physical instincts and lusts in the service of reason and conscience, to deny himself and his natural selfishness that

he may minister to others ; and, in a word, a
creature capable of rising out of the necessities
of mere physical law by obeying what St. James
calls "the law of liberty" because it can only
be freely obeyed.

Here, then—whether by evolution or any
other process matters not a jot—we not only
find spirit in man and confess it to be his
supreme endowment, we also see that nature
itself is so ordered and conditioned that it is for
ever mounting to higher forms and freer modes
of existence; and that, in its advance toward
this spiritual heritage of freedom, it is for ever
suggesting an Intelligence, a Will, at work
behind it, which is seeking to raise and redeem
it into the liberty for which it yearns. If the
effect cannot be greater than its cause, must
not the Creator of the universe and the Maker
of man be a Spirit? Has not Moses reason
with him when he writes *God, God, God* across
the heavens and over the whole earth? If

science be a reasonable interpretation of the facts of nature, must not science herself confess, as she watches this wondrous ascent from bondage to freedom, from blank and blind subjection to intelligent and voluntary obedience, that a free intelligent Spirit is at work through the whole round of nature, and that its only adequate cause must be sought in God?

(12) But if we concede so much as this, can we refuse to concede far more? Whether or not Evolution be the last word and the master word of science, *we* are not bound to determine Some of her eminent disciples affirm that the evolutionary theory has been logically demonstrated; while others, equally eminent, contend that as yet it is no more than a probable hypothesis. It is a question which they must be left to determine for themselves; though, however they may determine it, we shall continue to hold that the final word is far from having been pronounced, and expect to witness

D

triumphs of scientific discovery in the future at
least equal to its victories in the past.   But
that, however it may be named, there has been
a long process of development in nature, a
gradual ascent from lower to higher forms of
life, and that this ascent culminates in man,
no one denies or can reasonably deny.   Why,
then, should this process, which has occupied
not only the centuries of human history, but
also the long æons of the geological record,
stop abruptly at the point which it has now
reached ?   Is it not far more rational to believe
that the process is still going on, the ascent
still culminating, the ladder still rising, however
slowly and imperceptibly, and that in future
ages and æons both man and nature will continue to develop into a perfection we cannot
as yet conceive?   But if that process is to go
on, who does not perceive that as hitherto the
whole realm of nature has been pressing on
and upward to produce the spirit of man, as in

that spirit we have the highest consummation
it has yet touched, so in that spirit we must
look for the starting-point of the new development? Here, in spirit, is the topmost point
nature has reached; if it is to rise higher still,
must it not start from this point? Must not
that which is *spiritual* in nature unfold new
energies, pervade and dominate that which is
material more fully, and perchance transform
it at last into its own quality and substance?
May not that great word of the Apostle, "first
that which is natural, and afterwards that which
is spiritual," be truer after all than any hypothesis which science has formulated, or any
generalization which philosophy has framed?

(13) The method by which this development
or advance has been effected is, we are told,
that of differentiation and individualization;
which means, I suppose, that when by some
happy conjunction of outward conditions with
inward organization a certain member of any

species grows to be different from and to excel its fellows, this happy variation, this favoured individual of the species, becomes the source from which a new species springs, the type to which it conforms. The line of advance runs through these selected and favoured organisms. For years, perhaps for ages, a lower type of life has waited for the happy moment in which its most perfect and richly endowed form should appear; and then, when it appears, this perfected form constitutes a new point of departure, and the process of development starts on its upward way once more.

If, then, when nature has risen into man, that process is still to go on, and to go on by this same method of differentiation, for what should we look? We should look, not for any abrupt rise in the whole level of human life, but for the selection of favoured individual forms, *i.e.* for elect men, who shall be raised by some happy conspiracy of outward conditions and inward organization above the common level, into higher and ever higher forms of life, until at last the one Supreme Man is born in whom the whole laborious ascent is consummated, and from whom there may spring men of a higher species, of a type answering to his own.

This is what science herself teaches us to expect as we follow "the struggle of existence from dim nebulous beginnings" to ordered worlds, and from the lower forms of animate life up to the dawn of consciousness and the rich personal life of man. And what science has taught us to expect is precisely that which the Bible declares the great creative and re-deeming Spirit to have done. For what, after all, is the story which the Bible has to tell but this; that when the common plane of humanity had been reached, by a process of natural selection Abraham and his seed were differen-tiated from their fellows, elected to special favour, raised to a higher type, set apart to be

a peculiar people of happier spiritual conditions
than the other races of mankind; that from
this selected and highly favoured stem, illustrated all along by the noblest types of human
life, there broke at last the peerless and con-
summate flower of humanity, a Man so perfect
as to present a new and higher type of man-
hood; and that from Him, the perfect Son of
Man, there has sprung and is ever springing a
new and higher order of men, spiritual rather
than natural men, born from above as well as
from below, one with Him already, but ever—
on both sides of the gate of death—pressing
on to a closer likeness, a fuller participation of
his Divine life; so that the very Apostle who
declared the divine order to be " first that which
is natural, and afterward that which is spiritual,"
also affirms the first man to have been of the
earth earthly, while the second man is the Lord
from heaven ?

In fine, Science and the Bible are at one

and will be seen to be at one whenever scientific men learn to treat the Bible fairly, and religious men learn to deal fairly with the discoveries of Science. They both proclaim a spiritual Cause of the world, and a spiritual End for it. They both affirm that nature is from Spirit, by Spirit, for Spirit. They both teach that as all things come from God, so also things tend to God and will reach their true goal and perfection as they return to and rest in Him, the Alpha and Omega, the First and the Last, the Beginning and the End.

CHAPTER II.

THE PROBLEM STATED.

(14) AFTER the unfounded assumption that the Bible affirms a genesis of the world which is demonstrably unscientific, there is no point on which modern sceptics lay more stress than the undoubted fact, that the Bible records signs and wonders which imply a power above nature, if not against it. Perhaps the objection would be more accurately stated were they to say, that the miracles of the Bible imply the activity, in nature, of a Power of which our modern scientific interpretation of nature finds no trace. But, state the objection how we may, it is a formidable one, and has done much to unsettle

the faith both of those who still believe, and of those who once believed, the Bible to be or to contain the word of God.

Now so long as the Church conceived of miracles as violations of the laws of nature, it was very natural, and even reasonable, that sceptics should declare miracles to be impossible: for how should God transgress his own laws? or how can any purely physical law be broken? But now that the Church conceives of miracles as modifications of the ordinary course of nature, induced by the coming in of a higher force acting on a higher law, sceptics no longer pronounce miracles to be impossible indeed, but they still declare them to be incredible. How can they pronounce them impossible when even they themselves possess and wield a power by which the ordinary course of nature is constantly modified and overruled? When, to use a familiar illustration, I fling a stone into the air, I do not violate the law of gravitation ; I simply modify, and to a certain extent override, its action by bringing a new force into play, that of my own will. The intelligence and will of man have changed the face of the whole earth. By hewing down forests, by ploughing and draining fields, by laying down roads and railroads, by building houses, cities, dykes, harbours, ships, we have not only modified the surface of land and sea, we have also invaded the kingdom of the air, and changed the very climates on which, in large measure, the life of nature depends. There is not a single square inch in England, probably there is not a square inch in the whole world, which is to-day what it would have been had it been left to the free play of purely natural forces. But if the will of man has so largely modified the action of these forces, who can doubt that the will of God might, should He, for some worthy end, think fit, modify it much more widely, subtly, and potently ?

(15) " No," says the modern sceptic, "miracles are not impossible, if by miracle you mean simply a modification of the natural order by the introduction of a supernatural force, and if I admit that any such supernatural force exists. But though they are not impossible, they are incredible ; for no adequate reason for them has ever been adduced, nor have they been submitted to the scientific tests by which alone they could be verified."

And if in our turn we ask : How, then, do you account for the fact that in a Book, confessedly the greatest and noblest in the literature of the world, and by men who seem to be very honest and competent witnesses, miracles are constantly affirmed, and are so blended with both the theology and the morality they taught —their theology, moreover, being the highest, and their morality the purest the world has ever seen—that the one cannot be disentangled from the other? The sceptic replies : " The miracles of the Bible can and must be disentangled from its teaching. They are late and legendary additions to it. They are of the nature of those myths which we find in the earlier stages of the history of every race, the fabulous inventions with which every race glorifies its own origin, its own founders and heroes. The growth of such myths implies no insincerity ; the allegation is not that they are wittingly or wilfully fabricated. Great teachers, warriors, rulers, benefactors, naturally live on in the memory and affection of their fellows long after they are dead. Their achievements are exaggerated, their character exalted, first by affection, then by tradition, till they grow to be of more than mortal stature ; a halo gathers round their brows, and they are worshipped as gods, or at least as sons of the gods, while the far-resounding echoes of the great deeds they really did swell into monstrous and fabulous proportions."

And such a reply does not, at the first blush, seem to be unreasonable. It falls in with many vague notions which are floating in our minds, and comes to us with all the added strength which these vague notions lend it. It is only when we bring it to the Bible, and try to read the Bible in its light, that we discover how utterly this plausible hypothesis breaks down. For there we find both that the miracles of the Bible cannot possibly be disentangled from its teaching, and that these miracles bear no single trace, mark, or note of the legendary growth or mythical invention to which they are ascribed.

(16) That the miracles of the Bible cannot be detached from its theology and morality has been proved again and again, and proved most conclusively; for the sceptical argument has been broken down not at its weakest, but at its strongest, point. How often of late years, for example, and from how many quarters, have

we been admonished to drop the supernatural
and even the theological element in the Gospels,
and to content ourselves with the pure, sweet,
and lofty morality of the Sermon on the Mount ;
on which Sermon those whom we call sceptics
have lavished eulogies so nobly conceived and
so eloquently expressed that it would be hard
to match them from the writings of apologists
and divines.   But if for a moment we accept
their advice and confine ourselves to the Sermon
which, for them, sums up all that is most valuable in the Gospel of Christ, do we thereby
exclude either theology or miracles from our
field of view?   On the contrary, not only do
we find in this Sermon a doctrine of God, a
doctrine of the Holy Ghost, a doctrine of Providence, a doctrine of Sin and of the Forgiveness
of Sins, a doctrine of Prayer, and a doctrine
of Heaven, but we also find that the motives
to which its pure and lofty morality appeals
are purely theological motives.   We are to do

good, hoping for nothing in return ; we are to give alms without advertising them ; we are to love all men, even our enemies ; we are to requite good for evil and give a blessing for a curse ;— not from any merely ethical motive, but from purely religious motives, that we may please our Father who seeth in secret, that we may prove ourselves to be his children, that we may become perfect even as He is perfect. We are not to be careful, because our Father careth for us ; we are to forgive, because He has forgiven us ; we are to ask for what we want, because our Father knows how to give us his good gifts ; and we are not to be importunate in our prayers, because our Father knoweth what we have need of before we ask Him. In short, the whole round of motives in this Sermon is purely theological.*

But *the motives* of any ethical system are its essence ; they mould its character, they deter-

* Cf. "The Foundations of Faith," by Rev. Henry Wace, D.D.

mine its quality. How, then, can we detach
the theology of the Sermon on the Mount from
its morality when, to do that, would be simply
to detach the motive from its every precept,
to rob it of its essence, and so to destroy its
very existence ?

And as for detaching miracles from this
Sermon, that is wholly impossible, except at the
cost of vitally impairing its integrity. For not
only does it imply a supernatural element
throughout, but in the verses in which it culminates—verses than which none are more dear to
the sceptic and the moralist, if only because they
rebuke the hypocrisy of the Church—our Lord
represents some of his followers as claiming to
have wrought miracles, nay, as having really
cast out devils in his name, and in his name
done many wonderful works ; and as, nevertheless, being rejected by Him because they had
not cast the devil out of their own heart, but
had been workers of iniquity as well as workers

of miracles. And yet how should He have spoken of them as working miracles, and working them in his name, if He himself did no miracle? How should his mere Name have been so potent if He Himself exercised no supernatural power?

No, we can no more detach miracles than we can detach theology from the Sermon on the Mount. And if miracles, theology, and morality are inextricably blended in the very Sermon which the opponents of theology and miracles have selected as their battle-field, and which they so love and admire that they would fain reduce the whole teaching of Christ to the limits of this single discourse, we may be sure that in the other sections and books of the Bible miracles and teaching are still more obviously, if not still more intimately, intertwined.

(17) That the miracles of the Bible present none of the well-known notes or marks which characterize the myths of other ancient scrip-

tures or traditions becomes apparent as soon as we study them, and especially as we observe the manner in which they are distributed through its pages. These marks are so well known, so generally admitted, that I need only enumerate them.

Myths, then, belong to the earlier reaches of human history, and tend to disappear as we come down the stream of time.

Myths tend to glorify a race or the origin of a race, and the great men who have illustrated and adorned it.

Myths take time to grow ; if no man is a hero to his own valet, so also no hero or prophet is exalted to divine honours by his own generation or in his own age and land.

I do not pause to argue these points. They are admitted axioms. But if we apply these axioms to the Bible story, fairly yet firmly, we are likely to be at once surprised and edified by the result.

(18) The first fact likely to strike a student of the Bible who seeks to acquaint himself with the story it tells is that, whereas in all other literatures myths abound in the earlier stages of history and gradually disappear as that history comes into clearer light, in the Bible we absolutely have no record of a single miracle, a single indubitable modification of natural laws by a supernatural power, for the first twenty-five centuries of the space it covers! Creation is of necessity miraculous on any theory of it, and hence no candid reader will affect surprise at finding certain marvellous displays of supernatural energy in the document which records the creation of the world and of man. But if, as we are bound to do, we refuse to reckon as a miracle any event, however marvellous, which can be fairly attributed to natural or secondary causes—as, for example, the Deluge or the destruction of the Cities of the Plain—we are met by this most remarkable fact, that from the creation of the

world down to the call of Moses, a period of two
thousand five hundred years, the laws of nature
hold on the even tenour of their way, unbroken
by a single interruption, although these twenty-
five centuries, since they are the earliest in the
human story, ought, according to the mythical
hypothesis, to be the richest in tales of wonder.
Abraham wrought no miracle, nor Isaac, nor
Jacob, though these three patriarchs were the
venerated fathers and founders of the Hebrew
race, never forgotten in after years, never men-
tioned but with honour and pride ; and although
it is precisely the founders of a race with whom
tradition and mythical invention are most busy,
and round whose heads a legendary halo most
naturally gathers.

With the call of Moses, indeed, the first
miraculous epoch opens ; there commences an
extraordinary outburst of supernatural force ;
and so long as the sacred historian is narrating
the exodus from Egypt, the wanderings in the

Wilderness, and the entrance into the Promised Land, signs and wonders meet us almost on every page. Here, then, the mythical theory may seem to win an easy triumph ; for, confessedly, the origin of a race is apt to be glorified by legends which will not bear a critical examination. But this apparent triumph is turned into utter defeat the moment we mark that the miracles which attended the commencement of the national life do *not* glorify either Moses or the men whom he redeemed from their bondage and welded into a nation. So far as they were vouchsafed to Moses personally, they came, as we shall see, to compel him to an errand on which he was unwilling to go ; so far as they were wrought by Moses for the people, they were wrought in vain, and were the reproach of the nation rather than its glory.

The first two miracles in his personal record are those of the staff turned into a serpent and of the hand smitten with leprosy. Have these miracles, both of which attended his call to the service of God and of Israel, the look of myths invented by fond tradition to do him honour? What they really illustrate is his weakness, not his strength, his well-nigh invincible obstinacy and unbelief. It was because he would not go on the errand on which he was sent, because he could not be persuaded that he was competent for the task to which he was called, that these marvels were wrought. Even when they had been wrought, the historian tells us that he persisted in his obstinate reluctance and unbelief, until the anger of God was kindled against him. Is that in the tone of one who was inventing a mythic halo for the head of the Redeemer and Lawgiver of Israel, and who wanted to make him glorious in our eyes?

In like manner the miracles of the Wilderness, almost without exception, tell to the shame, not to the honour, of the men who, in the language of one of their own poets, there saw God, tempted

Him, and proved his work. Forty years long
was He grieved with them and provoked, working miracles only to still their murmurs, to
quench their mutinies, to repair their mistakes,
to rebuke their sins. Is it so much as con-
ceivable that miracles such as these were invented
by the poets of Israel in order to glorify their
origin, to give dignity and heroic splendour
to the men from whom they sprang? Or were
they so clumsy that, intending to lift their
fathers to heaven, they unwittingly cast them
down into this hell of opprobrium, folly, obstinacy, and flat rebellion against the Hand which
fed and guided them? That, surely, is a curious
example of the patriotic legend which, instead
of setting forth the fathers and founders of a
race as heroes and half divine, stigmatizes them
as such incurable and stiff-necked sinners that
the whole generation of them perished by and
for their crimes in the Wilderness !

No sooner were the Jews led through the

Wilderness and established in the Holy Land
by Moses, and Joshua his minister and successor,
than the display of miraculous power begins to
decline, and for a period of six centuries we
meet with only a dubious miracle here and
there. In the long picture gallery of Holy Writ,
no men have a more legendary look than the
border chieftains who rose to be Judges in
Israel. The age of the Judges is confessedly
the heroic age of the Hebrew chronicles; and
heroes are the very men round whose memories
marvels, legends, fabulous exploits, most naturally collect. The Judges were succeeded by
the Kings; and for whom should tradition weave
its mythical wreaths, or exhale its bright magni-
fying mists, if not for Saul the warrior, for
David the poet and darling of Israel, and for
Solomon its sage? In these three we have
the very style of man that attracts legends to
himself as by a natural law—as indeed they
have attracted them in chronicles less sober

than those of the Bible. And yet in the era
of the Judges only a few miracles are found,
while in that of the earlier and nobler Kings
they are altogether wanting.

It may be said, however," Miracles are not to
be looked for in an age so enlightened as that of
David and Solomon, when the Hebrews were
brought into contact with other races and higher
civilizations than their own ; an age of com-
merce, literature, art, in which knowledge grew
from more to more." How, then, are we to
account for the fact that, two centuries later,
we come on another extraordinary manifesta-
tion of the miraculous energy? Samuel
founded the schools of the prophets indeed ;
but Elijah and Elisha seem to have been the
men who first made prophecy a real and great
power in Israel, who brought its broader theology and loftier moral ideal to bear on the
national conscience. And with the advent of
Prophecy to power there came a whole series

of miracles as marvellous as any of which we read in the earlier and darker ages. At a period so late, and in a light so clear as to leave little scope for legend, we find marvels as numerous as ever, and as wonderful. Nor have these later marvels any trace of mythical invention upon them. Some of them illustrate the Prophet's weakness rather than his strength, tend to his shame, not to his glory, as, for instance, the miracle by which Elijah was fed in the Wilderness, after he had prayed that he might die rather than be sent back to a task so lonely and so hopeless; while all of them tend to the shame, rather than to the glory, of the people of Israel, since they were wrought to recover them from their idolatries and sins to the service of God, and wrought, as the poets and chroniclers both confess, almost wholly in vain. Nor, again, is it to his miracles that Elijah owes his grandeur and the large heroic proportions he assumes in our thoughts, but

to his character, to his indomitable courage, his
passionate loyalty and devotion ; just as Elisha
stands in our imaginations as the type of all
that is sweet, genial, gracious, in the man of
God, not because he did many mighty works,
but because his works, like those of One
greater than himself, were works of mercy and
compassion.

Once more the glory declines as these two
heroic figures pass from the scene, and the light
of the miraculous Shechinah is involved in the
cloud. And, now, we might well think the
world was growing too old and too wise to
babble of legends, and to delight itself in the
wonders proper only to its childhood. Four
centuries pass, illuminated only at scattered
and distant points by the supernatural efful-
gence. The national existence of the Jews has
come to an end. The land, once so populous
and thriving, lies desolate. Of a people, once
so mighty, only a few poor captives are left,

who sit and weep by the waters of Babylon. And here, of all places, at Babylon, fertilized by the waves of successive Eastern civilizations, among a people the most fierce, luxurious, and polished, the miraculous energy breaks forth once more, and Daniel and his compeers are so visibly guarded and taught by Heaven as to assure the dejected captives that God has not forgotten them, and to constrain the mighty Persian conqueror to unloose their chains and to send them back to the land of their fathers in peace. Yet even now this strange story tells against, rather than for, the people for whose redemption these marvels are wrought. Only an inconsiderable remnant of them respond to the heavenly call, and return to recommence their national life. Most of them reject the counsel of God against themselves, and fade out of history, absorbed by the races amongst whom their captivity has been spent; insomuch that the fate of ten

out of the twelve tribes remains, unto many, a
problem to this day. Still, therefore, the
miracles wear the same unmythical stamp.
They are not legends which any race would
have invented in its own honour. They proclaim its shame rather than its glory. For
which of these later prophets did not the Jews
reject or persecute? against which of these
gifted and patriotic statesmen did they not
rebel?

(19) In the minds of many readers this strange
story, so far as it has yet gone, the story which
the Bible tells of its own miracles, will, I
imagine, awaken some surprise. For most of us
have assumed that miracles are pretty evenly
distributed through the pages of the Old Testament, and thus we have missed the obvious
intention which goes far to vindicate and explain
them. When we see that its miracles group
themselves in three periods far removed from
each other, and cluster round three events of

prime importance, viz. the inception of the
national life, the advent of the Prophetic power,
and the redemption from the Babylonian captivity, we begin to get glimpses of a certain
Divine purpose, a certain Divine order and
propriety in them. We feel that, if God so
loved men as to reveal Himself and his will
to them when they could not find Him out,
and were perishing for lack of that knowledge
in which eternal life consists, it was natural that

He should elect one out of the various races
of men, and so manifest Himself to them as to
train and prepare them to receive, and to impart,
a growing revelation of his will. At the very
lowest we see that there was a certain economy,
such as characterizes all Divine works, in this
selection of one race to receive the supernatural
disclosure which was intended for the benefit
of all races ; while in the fact that the miracles
group themselves round the three critical points
in the history of that elect race, we recognize

a new illustration of that same economy of Divine power. Supernatural interventions are not lavished in unnecessary and wasteful profusion. They come only at the call of need. There is a certain unity in them. They conspire together for one great and worthy end; they are meant to reveal God as the Father, Teacher, and Saviour of mankind. Even with this end in view, the laws of nature are not unnecessarily and perpetually modified. Only at long intervals, only to usher in some great birth of time, does the Creative Spirit look through the veil of secondary causes, only "at sundry times," and to meet some pressing necessity, does the light shine through the cloud in which it is ordinarily involved.

If, then, we listen, as we are bound to listen, to the story told by the Bible itself, and mark the law which governs the distribution of its miracles, the haze of difficulty which enshrouds them thins, in large measure it lifts and disappears; and we can but confess that here, as everywhere else, God has revealed his will in a manner worthy of Himself.

(20) Even yet, however, the story is not fully told.   The best is still to come.

Another wide interval, an interval of four centuries, is placed between the Restoration from the Captivity and the advent of our Lord Jesus Christ ; and during these four hundred years no miracle is recorded, and even the voice of Prophecy is dumb. But when, "in the fulness of the times," the Son of Man appeared to redeem the world from a more dreadful captivity than that of Babylon and Egypt, and to complete the revelation of God as the Teacher and Saviour of mankind, it was but natural that the miraculous energy, which had emphasized each of its previous initiatory stages, should break forth and shine with a splendour beyond all precedent. If there was ever a moment in the history of man in which the Creative Spirit

might be expected to disclose Himself in works
natural to Him but supernatural to us, works
in which that Divine force, his sovereign and
almighty Will, should so modify the laws of
nature and of human nature as to compel
recognition, if not faith,—was not this such a
moment? Whatever our private verdict, however, the Gospels steadily affirm that when the
Son of Man, Himself the great miracle of time,
manifested Himself to Israel, He wrought among
them signs and wonders such as man had never
witnessed before, and that He communicated
this strange power to the men who "companied
with him."

Now if we recall these familiar miracles, and
ask ourselves whether they bear a single mark
of a mythical or legendary origin, we cannot
in candour deny that they are free from every
trace of it, despite all the attempts of keen
and erudite critics to fasten that colour upon
them. Myths belong to the earlier stages of

F

history; but this was the last stage in the
national history of the Jews. Myths tend to
glorify a race, or the great men of a race; but
the Jews rejected Him to whom these miracles
are ascribed; and, so far from placing Him
among their greatest, they hate and deny Him
to this day as a traitor and an apostate who
brought shame and disaster on the blood from
which He sprang. Myths take time to grow;
but the miracles attributed to the Son of Man
were attributed to Him in his lifetime, and were
recorded by his own cotemporaries.

We are told, indeed, that that age—late as
it was, and albeit we have derived from it
and the ages which immediately preceded it,
all that is highest and best in the civilization
of our own time—was a credulous age, in
which legendary and marvellous achievements
were freely ascribed to every personage who
attained an heroic stature. But with what
reason can we call that a credulous age in

which the mythologies and legends of the great Pagan superstition were all crumbling into dust, when the Epicurean philosophy took the very tone adopted by our modern materialists, and the Stoic anticipated the very maxims insisted on by our modern advocates of a rational morality uncomplicated by the dogmas of theology?

(21) If any man objects : "But we are speaking of *Jews*, not of Greeks and Romans ; and surely the Jews of that time were credulous and prone to see miracles where no miracles were?" we need not insist, in reply, on a fact for which there is nevertheless much evidence, viz. that even the Jews were deeply infected in the time of Christ, and for two or three centuries before that time, with the sceptical philosophy of Greece and Rome. There is an answer to it so conclusive that, though it has often been adduced, it has never been met, nor am I aware of any attempt even to refute

it. For at this very age there lived a man who
answered much more closely to the popular,
and even to the Jewish, idea of a hero than
Christ Jesus ; a man, moreover, who made a
far deeper impression on the imagination and
memory of his fellows ; and yet no miracle was
ever attributed to him, whether in the Bible or
out of it. John the Baptist was a Jew. ¶The
Jewish people recognized in him a prophet and
more than a prophet. They would gladly have
accepted him as the Christ. So profound was
the impression he made that "all Jerusalem and
all Judea went out after him ; " so profound that
Josephus, who dismisses Jesus with a single
dubious sentence, has much to say of the
character and mission of the stern unbending
seer and moralist, who struck his cotemporaries
rather as an embodied and inspired voice than
as a man of like passions with themselves.
And yet no legend has gathered round this
strange impressive figure, no halo gleams on his

brow. Neither his own disciples nor the Jewish people, nor Josephus or any other writer of his time, credits him with the supernatural power so freely ascribed to Jesus, and even to the meanest of his followers. So marked was the contrast between John and Jesus, that even the outlandish folk of Peræa were struck with it, and exclaimed, "John did no miracle, but all that John said of this man is true." It is, therefore, to beg the whole question, it is to evade rather than meet the point in dispute, when certain critics ascribe the miracles of Jesus to the credulous and myth-making tendencies of the age in which He appeared, although the most prominent and popular Jewish prophet of that age stands before us untouched by any ray of miraculous glory. Till this fact has been explained, this problem solved, we are hardly called upon to adduce any other argument against those who would reduce the wonders attributed to Christ to the level of worn-out and incredible myths,

(22) Yet there is another argument of no small weight. For, in the case of Christ, myths had no time to grow. It is true that sceptical critics have attributed our four Gospels to the middle or end of the second century. But it is also true that they have been led to affix this late date to them mainly by a desire to discredit them, and to leave room for the fabrications of myths. And it is still further true that they are now beginning to confess, that the Gospels must have been written at a much earlier date than they once supposed. Into this long and difficult controversy, however, we need not enter. For here again we can appeal to a fact which has never been denied, never seriously questioned even. The most sceptical critics admit that four of St. Paul's Epistles— I and 2 Corinthians, Romans, Galatians—were written by the Apostle whose name they bear. But St. Paul was born, as they also admit, in about the same year as our Lord. He wrote

these Epistles within twenty or thirty years of the death on the cross. In these Epistles he ascribes miracles and miraculous powers to our Lord as clearly and emphatically as do any of the men who wrote the Gospels. He tells us that he had affirmed these miracles from the moment of his conversion; nay, that his own conversion was due to a miracle. Here, then, we have the testimony of one who was of the same generation with Christ—a testimony which leaves no time or scope for the invention of legends, for the growth of myths.

And what need we more? Are we to doubt St. Paul's testimony simply because he was a Christian? But he was not *always* a Christian. He had hated and persecuted Christ. What made him a Christian except that he could not resist the power which conquered even his stubborn and ardent antagonism? His conversion, fairly weighed, does but give new force to his evidence.

(23) At every point, therefore, the mythical hypothesis breaks down, although in some form this hypothesis is the only explanation of the Biblical miracles which the sceptical criticism of the day offers us. If we ask the Bible for its own account of its own miracles, it tells us that, instead of being common and constant, they are rare ; that they come only at wide intervals, and to usher in some new and momentous epoch. It groups them round the commencement of the national and religious life of Israel, the advent of Prophecy to power, the redemption from the Captivity, and the coming of that great Prophet, like unto Moses, who was sent to give life to the whole world and to redeem all men from their bondage to vanity and corruption.

(24) Now, obviously, before we can attempt to *solve* the problem of miracles with any hope of success, we must *state* that problem : we must get the statement of the Bible itself. And

in addition to all we have yet learned from the Bible, as a corollary or inference from all that we have yet learned, the Bible affirms that the four miraculous epochs in the history of man mark four successive and ascending stages in God's revelation of Himself and of his will to the world. The need for such a revelation needs no proof. That man by searching cannot find out God, even in such poor "perfection" as is possible to man, is surely put beyond a doubt by the moral and religious confusion to which the world, after a search of so many centuries, was reduced at the advent of Christ. In proportion as any man is familiar with the moral and religious conditions of that age, he will admit, what Plato anticipated, that nothing short of a Divine self-revelation could have raised men from the shame and bondage of the pit into which they had fallen. And the affirmation of the Bible is that the revelation thus given in the person, teaching, and work of our

Lord Jesus Christ was one for which long and patient preparation was necessary, and had been made; that *one* race had to be, and had been trained century after century to receive and to disseminate it; that the miraculous epochs of which we have spoken were necessary parts of that training; that at each of these epochs a new and higher form of revelation was introduced; that miracles were necessary and were designed to compel attention to and illustrate the new stage, the loftier moral ideal, which had been reached, and to raise the chosen race from the lower stage which it had long occupied, and to which it had grown familiar and attached; and that in the fulness of times, when this training was complete—and, as it seems to us, long before it was complete—God sent forth his Son to make a final disclosure of his will, to fulfil and make good all which those who came before Him had promised and fore-shadowed.

Now the true statement of any problem is an immense aid to the solution of it. And already, although as yet the statement of our problem is not complete, I think it must be admitted that it has grown simpler and easier to us ; that there is a certain harmony and consistency in all that we have heard the Bible say of its own miracles which is very reassuring, and which does much to relieve the problem of the difficulties and improbabilities that our false·or partial statements of it have attached to it. Does not the Bible, when duly examined, set forth a worthy and sufficient end for the miracles it records ? Does it not set them forth in a natural and noble sequence? If miracles are possible, can such miracles as these be altogether incredible, at least to those who believe in God and in any revelation of his will ?

(25) To complete our statement of the problem, it only needs that we briefly glance at the miracles which accompanied the final

or Christian stage of the Biblical revelation,
and gather up what it has to say of the signs
and wonders ascribed to our Lord.

Consider, then, *the quality* of the miracles
attributed to Christ. So little legendary are
they in form and substance, that even the most
sceptical critics confess them to be the very
perfection of sober good sense when once they
are compared with the legends of the Hebrew
writings not contained in the Bible, or with
the marvels of any Pagan mythology which
we are able to recover. Where, for example,
do we meet in the Gospels with any "work"
which even descends toward the level of the
puerile fables which tell us how the boy Jesus
breathed the breath of life into birds which
He had moulded of clay, or that He gathered
up in his "napkin" the water He had spilled
from a broken jug?

Consider, again, how the miracles attributed
to Him harmonize with all that the New

Testament affirms of his nature, his character, his teaching. If, as the Gospels steadfastly assert, He was Himself a miracle, what more natural than that He should work miracles? If He was God as well as man, must not He shew forth the God in Him as well as the man? If He was only what He meant when He called Himself "the Son of Man," if, that is, He was only the ideal Man, might He not naturally possess a greater power over the forces and laws of nature than we do, who yet are modifying those forces and laws by every breath we draw, and every action we perform? Might He not well rise to that absolute dominion over all the works of God's hands which the ancient seers claimed as the proper, though forfeited, heritage of man? Might not He whose will was invariably at one with the will of God, be *trusted* with a power which could not safely be confided to us while our wills are so weak and variable and prone to

stray from their rest ?   If, only, He was without
sin, as many admit who pronounce his miracles
incredible or deny his " proper deity," was not
his very sinlessness the greatest of all miracles,
supposing Him to have been a man of like
passions with ourselves ?

And how came He to speak as man never
spake if He were not what man never was ?
Innumerable attempts have been made, indeed,
to reduce the peerless Son of Man to the level
of other great teachers of antiquity, attempts,
however, which even the ablest and most fear-
less sceptics—*e.g.* Goethe, Carlyle, John Stuart
Mill — have branded as utter and miserable
failures : but if we would measure the distance
between Him and them; we have only to compare the tone and bearing of Christ with those
of Socrates, or Plato, or even St. Paul. In
them we have ardent inquiry, lofty speculation,
an earnest devotion to the best and highest
aims of life, blended with a constant sense of

ignorance, failure, dependence, personal unclean-
ness; while in Him, and in Him alone, we
find from the first a calm that never wavers, a
wisdom that knows no bound, a holiness unconscious of a single spot, an authority unbroken
by a doubt.

Consider, too, how his teaching was illustrated by his "works"; how, by opening the
eyes of the blind, for example, He illustrated
the saying, "I am the Light of the world"; how,
by raising the dead, He proved Himself to be
"the Resurrection and the Life"; how, in short,
by healing the diseases of men and redeeming
them from their distresses, He proclaimed
Himself to be the Saviour of the world.

What would the Gospel be to us if there were
no forgiveness of sins? But He who forgives
sins modifies the action of great moral laws,
by bringing a new moral force into play; and
shall not He who can thus modify and override moral laws also modify and overrule

physical laws? Is it much that He who could
say, "Thy sins are forgiven," should also say,
"Take up thy bed and walk?"

Consider, once more, the *self-consistency* of
the Gospel miracles, how they all move in one
plane and work together for one end. The
Incarnation might be incredible to us if it
introduced an ordinary life; but the life of
Christ is an extraordinary one; through its
whole course it answers to the greatness of its
beginning. The resurrection and ascension of
Christ might be incredible if they closed an
ordinary career; but as the close of *his* career
on earth they seem simply natural and appropriate.

Glance at his miracles, moreover, in the
light of his mission, of the work He is yet to
do. According to the Scriptures of the New
Testament, He is to raise all men from the
dead, to judge or rule them all, to overcome
evil with good, to redeem the very creation

from its bondage to vanity and corruption, to subdue all things unto Himself; and, finally, to hand over to his Father a perfected universe. But if that is to be the crown and consummation of his work, is it unreasonable to expect that He who by a stupendous miracle, which involves the modification of all laws both physical and moral, is to reform and reconstitute the universe, should give us some signs and foretastes of his power even from the first?

(26) Now we have no right to detach this miracle and that from the whole series of his mighty works, or from all else that the Bible tells us of Him, all that it tells us of his character, his teaching, his claims, his mission, and final triumph, and consider them apart. We cannot so much as see them truly save as we see them in their full and natural connections. The whole thing hangs together, and we are bound to deal with it as a whole. And if we

G

thus deal with it, the mere Biblical statement
of the problem goes far toward solving it. For
taking it thus, we see that the Bible groups its
miracles round the great epochs in the religious
history of the race, each of these epochs pointing
to and preparing the way for the last, and all
culminating in the advent and work of Christ.
We see that the Bible claims for Him a nature
and character of which miracles would be a
natural outcome. We see that all his " works "
are good works ; that they illuminate the truths
He came to teach ; that they are consistent with
each other, as well as with his character and
teaching ; and that they are also consistent both
with the redeeming work He did on earth, and
the yet greater work which He has promised to
do from heaven. All the lines of the Divine
action and revelation in the past concentrate in
Him ; all their lines in the future ray out from
Him.

If we once accept this simple, but most wonderful story, it is nothing to say that the miracles of the Bible bear no trace of mythical or legendary invention; it is nothing to say that no other or later "marvels" are worthy to be compared to them. We may go further and say that the miracles of Christ become *credible* to us by their utter consistency with all else that the Bible contains ; that they commend themselves to us as natural and inevitable features of the great story it tells.

CHAPTER III.

THE PROBLEM SOLVED.

(27) Now that the ground has been cleared, as I would fain hope, by a statement of the problem, drawn from the Bible itself, which refutes the mythical theory of Miracles, it may be possible for us to approach our problem with some prospect of arriving at a reasonable and adequate solution of it. Not that the way is quite clear even yet. For our opponents, driven from the mythical theory, fall back behind the battery of Hume, and contend that, if not impossible, miracles are so incredible, so opposed to the course of nature and the teachings of experience, as that *no* evidence can substantiate

them, however honest or strong it may be. It is natural that they should betake themselves to this defence, for no other is any longer open to them. The critical argument, the attempt to prove, *e.g.* the late origin of the Gospels, and so to leave room for the mythical theory to work, has quite failed ; as indeed they themselves, by the mouth of their most eminent and eloquent representative (M. Renan, in his *Vie de Jésus*), have candidly confessed. Accordingly they fall back, as he falls back, on the assumption which led both Strauss and Baur to weave their exploded critical hypotheses, viz. that "what *could not* happen *did not* happen," and that miracles could not have happened because they are contrary to general experience ; * or, to state the objection in their own words : "Miracles, or the intervention of Deity in human affairs, are, to

---

* This point is wrought out at length, and with masterly ability, by Dr. Wace, in *The Gospel and its Witnesses*, chap. i. and ii.

the scientific thinker, *à priori*, so improbable, that no amount of testimony suffices to make him entertain the hypothesis for an instant."

This is the argument, or assumption, which we now have to meet. And I know not how better to approach it than by considering the words of the Roman Centurion as reported by St. Matthew (chap. viii. 8, 9), and pursuing the line of thought which they suggest; for, approaching it thus, we shall arrive, I trust, at a solution of our problem which is both reasonable and adequate, while we also expose the fallacy of the last assumption of modern scepticism.*

(28) "This heathen soldier," says Luther, "turns theologian, and begins to dispute in as fair and Christian-like a manner as would suffice

---

* The solution which I am about to offer is wrought out with the most admirable simplicity and force in a treatise *On the Difference between Physical and Moral Law* (the Fernley Lecture of 1883), by Rev. William Arthur, M.A., which appeared some months after this Essay was published. It was also presented, in a less complete form, in an essay on *Prayer*, which I contributed to *The Expositor* for 1877.

for a man who had been for many years a doctor
of divinity." It would not be difficult to go
beyond Luther, and say, This heathen soldier
reasons more fairly than many doctors of divinity
—more logically and conclusively even than
many philosophers and men of science, to whom
doctors of divinity are a very little thing. So
admirably does he dispute, that Jesus Himself
discovers in his arguments the inspirations of
faith, and declares with an accent of astonishment, "Verily, I have never found a faith so
great as this, no, not even in Israel!"

Not in Israel? No; for the Jews sought a
sign, and except they saw signs and wonders
they would not believe. But the Centurion, so
far from seeking a sign, declines one with gentle
humility, and can believe though no wonder be
wrought. "Heal my servant," he had cried, or,
in his own soldierly phrase, "Heal *my boy*." "I
will *come* and heal him," said Christ. "Come!"
replied the Centurion. "But there is no need

to come. The powers of sickness and of health,
all the forces of nature and of human nature,
are at thy command, just as my soldiers and
servants are at mine. I do not need to run on
every errand myself; nor do you. I am *under*
authority, and therefore I am *in* authority. I
represent the Imperial power I serve; and therefore I can say to my soldiers, Go, and they go,
or, Come, and they come; and to my servants,
Do this or that, and they do it. You hold a
commission from Heaven; and because you
are *under* Divine authority, you *have* a Divine
authority, and can send the forces of nature on
your errands and compel them to do your bidding. Speak the word only, and my boy will
be healed." Obviously he held that there was
an analogy between the ruler of the Roman
empire and the Lord and Governor of the
universe, between himself and the Son of Man,
and believed that Christ had such a delegated
authority over the forces and laws of nature and

of human life as he himself exercised over the men of his "century" and the servants of his household. In short, the poor man was guilty of a crime of which in all probability he had never heard—the crime of anthropomorphism— a vice in logic, a sin in morals, if at least we are to listen to those who, when they do not claim a monopoly of logic, assume a certain easy supremacy in the court of Reason.

For this ancient and simple view of God, of his power to use the forces and laws of nature in his service and in the service of man, and even to delegate to others such a power of using them, stands at the farthest remove from that which obtains among those who style them- selves the representatives of modern science and thought. They pronounce the Centurion and all who hold with him guilty of anthropomor- phism in accents which assume anthropomor- phism to be the one unpardonable sin. They affirm that we must on no account conceive

of God as such an one as ourselves—a very
different thing, be it remembered, from conceiving of Him as "*altogether* such an one as
ourselves "—or attribute to Him the qualities
and affections which we ourselves possess. We
can know nothing of Him, they assert, but that
which nature teaches; or, at most, we must
believe nothing of Him which is contrary and
opposed to the teaching of the natural world.
And as in that world we find simply physical
forces which work by immutable laws, we may
conceive of Him as like a force, or like a law,
but must not think of Him as like a man.
Miracles, therefore, are incredible, since it is
impossible that God should ever interfere with
the operation of immutable laws, laws which
cannot be broken or set aside. And Prayer
is as irrational as miracles are incredible; for
if we ask of God only those things which would
come to us in the common and established
course of nature, why need we ask for them?

and if we ask that which He could give only by changing that course, we ask what it is impossible for Him to grant.

So that we have to choose between two theories of God; the ancient theory, that of the Centurion, which represents the forces and laws of nature as the servants of God, who do his pleasure, hearkening to the voice of his word; to whom He can say, Come, and they come, Go, and they go, Do this or that, and they do it: and the modern theory which represents them as so far his masters that He cannot touch or modify them, cannot bend them to his will, or bid them run on his errands, no, not even on the gravest emergencies, not even in order to teach men the truths they most need to know, or to save them from the sins by which they are being destroyed.

(29) Which of the two theories shall we choose? It is natural for us to prefer that of our own time. Many do prefer it; many more

are so shaken by it that they can no longer rest in the simpler theory of a bygone age. Yet we shall do well to pause before we adopt this modern theory, although it loudly claims to be the product of pure reason, and denounces its venerable rival as utterly irrational. Not that we for a moment question the right of men unversed in theology to pronounce an opinion on even the most profound and momentous of theological questions. If a soldier of the ancient world might "turn theologian," and is to be admired for it, surely a modern man of science may also do so at least unblamed, and argue "like a doctor of divinity, if he will and can. But when he argues, and before he claims any monopoly, or any superiority, of sound reasoning, he should at least be careful to make his argument both consistent and conclusive. He should not contradict himself, or put it into our power to confute him out of his own mouth. Yet this, and nothing

less than this, is precisely what those do who
affirm that if we go to nature, and to nature
alone, for our conception of God, we shall admit
miracles to be impossible or incredible. Their
argument must have a certain plausibility, or it
would never have obtained so wide a vogue ;
it would neither be so constantly repeated by
as many as reject at least the supernatural
element of the Christian revelation, nor would
it have so seriously staggered the faith of many
who still accept that revelation. But no sooner
do we carefully examine it than we discover
it to be utterly unsound, and even in direct
and flagrant contradiction to the most cherished
convictions of the very men who advance it.

For consider what it is they really do. They
bid us go to the natural world for our ruling,
if not for our sole, conception of God and of
the manner in which He stands related to
human life and history. They say that we
must believe nothing of Him which is incon

sistent with the teaching of that world. And they infer that any miraculous intervention in human affairs is incredible because, the laws of nature being immutable, they can never be bent or broken or overruled. What, then, is this natural world to which we are referred? Is it the whole realm of nature, or only a part of it? It is, as we learn to our amazement, only a part of it, and an inferior part. It is the natural world *with man left out.* To base any conception of God on the nature of man, on his intelligence, conscience, affection, is to be guilty of anthropomorphism. *Matter*-morphism —if, to make my meaning clear, I may use such horrible compounds—is, it would appear, a quite virtuous and reasonable procedure; but *man*-morphism is utterly irrational and vicious. To think of God as like a natural force, or as like the law by which that force is governed, or even as a vague stream of tendency, is legiti- mate and praiseworthy; but to think of God

as like a man, even when man is at his best
and highest, is illegitimate to the last degree,
and cannot be too severely condemned.

Yet man has always been regarded as the
very flower and crown of nature; and we have
been taught by science herself to attach a value
to the human world, or even to any single
man in it, which outweighs that of the whole
material universe. Why, then, should it be a
sin against reason to frame our conceptions of
the Maker and Lord of the universe, at least
in part, from that which is highest in it and
most valuable? Should we not expect to get
our best conceptions of the Highest from that
which is confessedly the highest of his works?
If we may take up into our conception the
sense of force or power, and the sense of law
or order, which we derive from the inanimate
elements of nature, may we not also, and much
more, take up into it the intelligence, the
conscience, the affections which we find in her

animate elements? To refer us to the whole
sum of the natural world, and then to strike out
the chief factor—the human factor—of that
world; is not that plainly illogical, unfair
absurd?

(30) It is even more illogical and absurd now
than in any previous age. For, not to stoop
to the superstition of those who proclaim col-
lective Man to be the only true God, many of
our leading philosophers and men of science,
while they bid us omit man from the sum of
natural things, are teaching their disciples to
rejoice in that potent word *Evolution* as the one
key which unlocks all mysteries. *We* may
doubt whether it is more than a name for one
natural process out of many. We may ask
permission to suspend our verdict until we are
quite sure that no larger and higher law can
be discovered than a law which does nothing
to explain the origin whether of matter or
force, life or thought. But those who regard

the law of evolution as proved beyond all doubt,
and look down with superior scorn on as many
of us as hesitate to pronounce it the last best
gift of science, should at least remember that,
on their own theory, man is more essentially
than ever part, and the noblest part, of nature,
the consummation and epitome of the universe;
that in man nature presents us with the sum
and crown evolved by the age-long action of
the whole body of her forces and laws; and
that therefore, if nature had a Maker, we must
expect to find in man a more complete image
and reflection of his character than in any or
all other of the works of his hands. To say
that nature flowers in the reason and will, the
justice and love of man, and yet to contend
that, while we may and ought to take up into
our conception of God the suggestions of power
and order conveyed by the lower and inanimate
sphere of the universe, but are on no account
to take up into it any suggestion derived from

H

its upper and animate sphere, is a contradiction so obvious and absurd that it must be scouted as soon as seen. It is to say, and to say in the name of Reason, that nature does not include her own last and highest product! It is to say, and to say in the name of Reason, that she does not include the last evolution and the highest expression of the whole sum of her forces and laws! Theologians have many unreasonable assertions to answer for, many fallacious arguments; but it would be hard to find in any of their works an assertion more unreasonable or an argument more absurdly illogical than this.

In a word, science, which has so long condemned anthropomorphism as a sin, is now compelled to pronounce it a virtue. Instead of banning it as illogical and unsound, she can but bless it as the only sound and rational method open to us. For if we are to go to nature for our conception of God, and if man be "the

roof and crown of things," the last evolution
and highest expression of nature, where should
we go, if not to him, for our truest and best
conception of the Being who evolved him?
From what *we* are, we can learn most surely
what *He* is; from what *we* can do, we may
most surely infer what *He* can do. Under pain
of branding themselves as illogical and inconsis-
tent, those who make their boast in Evolution
must cease to sneer at anthropomorphism.

(31) But if, as science herself demands, we
turn to animate as well as inanimate nature, to
man as well as to matter, for our conception of
God and of his relation to us, mark how, not
only our doctrine of God, but also and mainly
the whole question of miracles changes its
form; and how the signs and wonders, so often
pronounced incredible, grow to be something
more than credible to us. To say that God
cannot interfere with the action of his own
laws, that He cannot so modify and overrule,

so hasten and retard their operation, as to produce what seem to us miraculous, *i.e.* strange
and wonderful, effects, is to say that He can
never do what man does every day :—which,
were it true, would perhaps in some measure
account for the fact that certain among us
worship Man rather than God. For, obviously,
man can, and does, both modify and overrule,
both hasten and retard, the operation of
natural forces and laws, and compel them in
a thousand different ways to produce effects
different from those which but for his inter-
ference they would have produced. Had man
never intervened, England would have been
parcel forest and parcel swamp to this hour,
with a very different climate therefore to that
which we now suffer or enjoy, and with a very
different *flora* and *fauna* from that which it now
possesses. In short, the physical conditions of
the whole country have been modified and
changed by the advent and will of man ; while

in America the face of a whole continent has passed through a similar change almost within the memory of living men.

But when we use such illustrations as these when we say* that "there is not a single square inch in England, probably there is not a single square inch in the whole world, which is to-day what it would have been had it been left to the free play of purely physical forces," we use illustrations too large and manifold to be easily embraced and thought out. If we would grasp the immensity and the infinite variety of the changes wrought in the natural order by the force and wit of man, we must select some more limited example. And, possibly we could have no more striking and convenient example than this ; that in almost every well-to-do house in England we have a long series of proofs, collected from almost every country under heaven, that the face of the whole land, and

* See p. 42.

even the face of the whole earth, has been changed in order to make that house what it is. When we go into and about such a house, what do we find? We find bricks brought from distant clay fields, stones dug from quarries still more distant, timbers from Norway or Sweden, marbles from Italy or Greece; carpets from Persian, Belgian, or Yorkshire looms; silks from India, China, or Japan; linen woven from Irish flax, and cottons from the Southern States of America; bread made from the wheats of Hungary, Russia, or the great Western States; coffee from the hills of Ceylon; rice from the swamps of Bombay or Italy; wines from France or Germany, Portugal or Spain; with a multitude of other necessary or precious things which it would be tedious to recount.

As we study the structure and contents of that one house, we feel that it is barely an exaggeration to say that the whole world has been taxed to build, furnish, and store it, and that the whole face of the earth has been changed in its service. For we must remember that hardly any one of the articles I have named would have been produced at all had the natural forces been left to take their own course, had they never felt the hand of man or submitted to his control. *Nature* does not make bricks, or carve stones, or polish marbles, or weave carpets, silks, linen, cotton, or broad-cloth, or make either bread or wine : of herself she cannot even grow a tea or a coffee which we should now deign to drink. All these things are monuments of the power of man, the trophies of his triumph over the forces and laws of the merely physical and inanimate world.

We must remember, too, that these pro-ductions imply the existence and activity of an immense array of cultivators, manufac-turers, merchants, artists, brokers, tradesmen, and handicraftsmen, each of whom modifies

the action of natural laws with every breath
he inspires, every step he takes, and whose
main function it is to modify the action of
natural forces, and compel them in countless
forms to serve his will.

And we must also remember that, in the
service of this one house, waggons are travelling
along every road, trains running on every
railway, boats plying on every river, ships
crossing every sea, messages flying along every
wire.

These, and the like, are the miracles, the
signs and wonders, wrought by Man; and
their name is Legion. By studying the forces
and laws of Nature, he has learned to modify
and control them; by serving, he rules them,
bending them, unbending and immutable though
they be, to the varying purposes of his will.
Why, then, should it be thought a thing incredible that God—if there is a God and He
is the Maker of men—should exercise a similar

and superior power over the forces and laws
of the material world? Why should not He
modify and control them far more subtly
and more effectively than the creature He has
made? He who created those forces, and gave
those laws, must not He know them more com-
prehensively and intimately than we do who
are still but stumbling over the very rudiments
of knowledge; and, knowing them so much
more perfectly, must He not be able to use
them with a corresponding perfection? We
touch them but from without; He from within.
And if, even with our imperfect knowledge of
them, and able only to lay a hand upon them
from without, we have nevertheless so far bent
them to our purpose as to harness them to
our service and change the face of the world,
what may not He do with them if He will;
if, that is, He sees some worthy end, as, for
example, the instruction or the salvation of
mankind, to be answered by so using them as

to disclose his presence, convey his thought, reveal his love? Signs and wonders as far above "the reaches of our souls," as our signs and wonders are beyond the comprehension of a savage or a child, are not and cannot be impossible to Him—if at least we may draw our conceptions of Him, as science herself bids us draw them, from nature as revealed in man, the flower and cream of the natural world. If *we* can say to its forces and laws, Do this, and they do it ; if we can bid them come and go on our errands ; shall not *He*, who formed both us and them, be able to do as much with them as we, and even more than we ?

(32) But many of our Lord's miracles, as also many of the miracles recorded in the Old Testament, were wrought on *men*, wrought to restore health to their bodies and sanity to their minds, to quicken them to the service and love of righteousness. And, therefore, if we would complete our argument, it is necessary

that, besides dwelling on the power of man over the physical world, we should at least glance at the immense power of man on men. To a reflective mind this latter power is far more wonderful, and often far more inexplicable, than the former ; and the difficulty of dealing with it lies in part in its subtlety, but still more in the vast range of example and illustration open to us. As a direct and consciously exercised power, it is wonderful enough ; but as an indirect and unconscious power, it is still more wonderful. History is full of examples, it is little more than a record, of the strange and marvellous influence on the fortunes of their fellows exerted by men of rare gifts and exceptional capacities. The sceptered dead still rule us from their graves. " Had there been no Luther," for instance, "the English, American, and German peoples would be thinking differently, would be acting differently, would be altogether different men and women from what

they are at this moment." *   Nor is the influence
of living men less remarkable. If use did not
blunt and stale our minds, it would be nothing
short of a perpetual marvel to us that from
this little island, with its comparatively few
inhabitants, no stronger and not much wiser
than their neighbours, one-fourth of the human
race, distributed over the whole globe, should
be governed and controlled, and the whole
human race be deeply influenced for good or
evil. It is hardly going too far to say that
the entire family of man, in all its branches,
through all its millions, listens with attention
to every public word that falls from the lips
of our Queen ; that an order from her sets the
whole world in · motion : and that no distinguished English statesman can make a
speech on any public question but that it
awakens echoes in every corner of the globe.
But it is still more wonderful, perhaps, that

* J. A. Froude, on *Luther,* in *The Contemporary Review* for
July, 1883.

a quiet thoughtful man, as yet unknown to
fame, with no army and navy to back him,
and no multitudinous array of servants to do
his bidding, cannot sit down to write a book
with a new thought in it, or that he cannot
discover some new law of science or some new
application of such a law, but that he too
shall set the whole world in commotion, change
and elevate the whole tone of civilized thought,
or effect a revolution over the whole surface
of civilized life. Such words and phrases as
Steam, Gas, the Telegraph, the Electric Light,
the Penny Post; Reform, Free Trade, Free
Press; the Conservation of Energy, the Con-
vertibility of Natural Forces, the Descent of
Man, and the Survival of the Fittest, sum up
in themselves the history of revolutions in the
mind and life of humanity which we owe to
men whose names might have been charged
with no memories and illustrious with no dis-
tinctions but for the several discoveries they

have made or advocated. Men less famous than these, or whose names the world has forgotten, have discovered drugs, or sanitary and healing methods and conditions of human life, by which some forms of disease have been extirpated, while other forms have been modified and impaired, and by which the general average of health and length of days has been extended and raised. And, still more strange, there have been, there are, men among us who, simply by the sweet and happy composition of their nature, or by their force of will, or by their power of penetrating to the secret springs of motive and desire, are able to minister to minds diseased, as well as to diseased bodies, and to restore health and harmony to those whose mental or nervous forces are like sweet bells jangled and out of tune.

Again, we have only to remember what a power Righteousness is in human life, insomuch that even the worst of men will rally round

a man admitted to be just, and admire in him
the purity and integrity which yet they themselves lack ; and what a power Love is, quickening even the dullest to a more vivid life, and
raising even the lowest to a higher life, to
become aware of the strange forces which are
hidden in our nature, of the singular and immense power which man may exert on man.

And if man can thus influence, heal, and
elevate his fellows, why may not God influence
men in a similar yet superior way ? why may
not those who are under his authority, and are
therefore called to exercise his authority? And,
above all, how can we pronounce it impossible
that He who, at least on the Christian hypothesis, was at once both man and God, should
influence, heal, and raise men far more subtly
and more potently than they influence each
other? If *we* tell upon each other for good
in proportion to our natural and acquired force,
in proportion to our wisdom, our righteousness,

our love, what must we expect and predicate of Him whose wisdom was without a flaw, whose righteousness was without a stain, and whose love knew no bounds ?

The Psalmist demands, " He that planted the ear, shall He not hear ? He that formed the eye, shall He not see ? " And surely we may continue the catechism and ask, " He that gave man brain and conscience, will and heart, shall not He think of us and care for us ? Shall He not be just? Shall He not love us and all men ? He that teaches men to control by serving his laws, shall not He control them ? He that gave them power to heal, shall not He heal ? He that calls them to teach and help, to serve and save each other, shall not He teach and help, serve and save us all ? " If we are to go to nature for our conception of God, we must go to man ; for man is the sum and crown of nature. And if we go to man for our conception of Him and of his relation to

us, who does not see that we must go, for our
conception of the Highest, to that which is
highest in man—to his will, his wisdom, his
justice, his love? Who will not admit that,
since man works a thousand signs and wonders
every hour, signs and wonders cannot be impossible to the Maker of men, that the forces
and laws of nature and of human life must be
far more perfectly under his control than they
are under ours?

(33) In arguing thus, I do not in the least
intend to cast any doubt on the fixity, the
steadfastness, of natural laws. Nor can I admit
the claim of modern men of science to be the
first to promulgate and insist on the stability
of these laws. In this as in much else, little
as they seem to know it, "doctors of divinity"
have anticipated them. The judicious Hooker,
for example,* died long before any one of them

* For the following quotation from Hooker I am indebted to
my friend Dr. Wace ; see his *Gospel and its Witnesses*, Lecture
vi., where he makes a very different but noble use of the passage.

I

was born ; but which of them has set forth the
immutability of natural law more statelily, im-
pressively, and musically than he has done in
a passage of his *Ecclesiastical Polity?* "If
nature should intermit her course, and leave
altogether, though it were but for a while, the
observation of her own laws ; if those principal
and mother elements of the world, whereof all
things in this lower world are made, should lose
the qualities which now they have ; if the frame
of that heavenly arch erected over our heads
should loosen or dissolve itself; if the celestial
spheres should forget their wonted motions, and
by irregular volubility turn themselves any way
as it might happen ; if the prince of the lights
of heaven, which now as a giant doth run his
unwearied course, should as it were through a
languishing faintness begin to stand and rest
himself; if the moon should wander from her
beaten way, the times and seasons of the year
blend themselves by disordered and confused

mixture, the winds breathe out their last gasp,
the clouds yield no rain, the earth be defeated
of heavenly influences . . . what would become
of man himself, whom these things do now all
serve ? See we not plainly that obedience of
creatures unto the law of nature is the stay of
the whole world ? "

No, we throw no doubt on the steadfast and
unchangeable action of the forces and laws of
nature. We do not assert that in working his
miracles our Lord either violated, suspended,
or abrogated them. All we affirm is that God
may, and that Christ did, use them in ways too
subtle and profound for us to grasp, yet in ways
not wholly unlike to those in which we ourselves
bend them to our service—using them to heal
the sick, and give sight to the blind, hearing
to the deaf, feet to the lame, and life to the
dying, or even to the dead. In short, we affirm
that He did perfectly and in full what even man
may do imperfectly and in part. And we affirm

it, we argue for it from premises which science herself has laid down, not only that the Bible miracles may be credible and reasonable to reasonable men—miracles which, as we have seen, are distributed through its pages with a singular economy, and are prompted by a motive so worthy, so divine; but also in order that we ourselves may believe that God, by secret ways past finding out—but which probably would be no whit more wonderful to us, if we could find them out, than our own control over the world and men—can still help, and heal, and save us; that He is not deaf to any of our prayers, or unable to answer them, but can still bestow wisdom and health, righteousness and love, on all who sincerely seek them at his hands.

(34) For, perhaps, the chief value of the Centurion's words lies in a suggestion which they still have to make to us: viz. that signs and wonders are not necessary or inevitable conditions, or concomitants, of miracles; but

that God, and the servants of God, may inter-
vene for our instruction, our recovery to health,
our salvation from every form of evil, even
though no singular or striking event should call
public attention to the work of power or of
grace.*

If we suffer his words to enter into "the
quick forge and working-house of thought," we
may behold the scene which with a few rapid
but graphic strokes he suggests. It is no
unusual, no unique, no miraculous scene to
which he points, but a scene of every-day life.
In the simple discharge of his duty as master
of a household, or as an officer in the Roman
army, he issues commands to his men and
servants, commands which they in their turn,
and as part of their ordinary duty, at once obey.
To this soldier he says, Go, and the man goes,

* "A miracle is not *a sudden blow struck in the face of nature,*
but a *use of nature,* according to its inherent capacities of service, by higher powers."—Newman Smyth, *Old Faiths in New
Light.*

and to that, Come, and the man comes: but had we seen his men moving through barrack or street at his command, we should have marked nothing strange in them, nothing to arrest attention, nothing even to denote the kind of errand on which they went, however singular that errand might have been in itself. And, in like manner, when he said to his servants, Do this, or, Do that, and they did it, had we beheld them as they went about house or market, we should have noticed nothing remarkable in their demeanour. Had we thought of them at all, we should simply have concluded that they were discharging the common household duties which fell to the servants of a man of his wealth and position. The level, matter-of-fact, matter-of-course tone which the Centurion maintains throughout his argument assures us that he was speaking only of the ordinary incidents of his life and vocation ; and that when he asks Christ to " speak the word

only, and my boy will be healed," he was simply
asking for what he conceived to be an ordinary
incident in *his* life and vocation.

Yet what an amazing leap it seems to us
from the one series of facts to which he alludes
to the other! Our Authorized Version omits
the "also" from St. Matthew's report of the
phrase, "I *also* am a man under authority";
and perhaps our Revisers have done us no more
notable service than in restoring the word to
its true place : for when one thinks of it, the
word fairly trembles and staggers under its load
of meaning. "I *also*"; "I *as well as you*"; "I
like you" : what an audacious feat it appears to
us that this heathen soldier should compare
himself, should *even* himself, as the Scotch say,
to the Lord of glory ; how it astonishes us that
a man so humble should yet be so bold! For
what he really means and implies is nothing
less than this : "As I hold a commission from
Cæsar, so you hold a commission from God,

Because you are under his authority, you wield
his authority. All the forces and laws of
nature and of human life are at your command
because they are at his command. Even as
they go about their ordinary work, they do his
will; and they will run on your errands as they
run on his. You need not come to my poor
house and strike your hand over the palsied
and trembling limbs of my poor boy. Speak
the word only, give the order, utter the command, and it will be obeyed as surely and as
quietly as my soldiers go on my errands and
obey my word."

This was the Centurion's conception of God
and of his relation to the realm of nature; and
nothing can be plainer than that he conceived
of the natural forces and laws as *always* doing
the will of God, however quietly or secretly they
went on their several paths, however usual and
ordinary their tasks. Nothing can be plainer
than that he believed that one who was clothed

with God's authority could also command them, and would be obeyed by them as simply and as promptly as God Himself. Nothing can be plainer than that he thought miracles *natural* in a miraculous personage, the ordinary and inevitable incidents and consequents of a Divine vocation or commission ; and even that he held a miracle to be more and not less miraculous if it were wrought without pomp or show, without arresting attention or compelling astonishment.

And what we have specially to mark is, that this is not only the Centurion's conception of God and of his relation to the universe, but that it is also Christ's. For Christ Himself emphatically adopts it. In the face of this narrative it is vain for any man to contend, as some have contended, that though miracles have been freely attributed to the Son of Man, yet He Himself with his sane intellect, his sweet reasonableness and clear veracity, never claimed miraculous power. He claims it here. When

Jesus had heard how the Centurion conceived of Him and of his authority, He "marvelled, and said to them that followed, Verily, I say unto you, I have not found so great faith, no, not in Israel." And we know what *He* meant by "faith." To Him faith was the eye and the hand of the soul, the faculty by which men come to know things as they are in themselves, by which they behold and grasp the eternal facts and verities that underlie the shows of time. He approved, therefore, the Centurion's mode of conceiving God and God's power over the natural world; He adopted it and made it his own. It comes to us clothed with his authority who spake as never man spake, and to whom even those who resent and condemn all faith in miracles defer as at least the wisest and best of men, the greatest teacher of truth the world has ever seen.

So that in choosing between the two theories of which I spoke at the outset, the ancient

simple theory and the modern sceptical theory,
we really have to decide between the authority
of Christ, who was not of an age but for all
time, and that of men who claim, although their
claim is traversed by scientists as learned and
able as themselves, to be the representatives of
modern science and thought;* that is to say,

* As from the space they contrive to fill in the public eye,
and the confident tone in which they address the public ear,
many young and ignorant people are under the impression that
the sceptical and materialistic school embraces most of the real
leaders or most eminent professors of science, it may be worth
while to jot down as they occur to me the names of a few of the
eminent men of science who cannot see "the promise and the
potency of all things " in matter, but, on the contrary, maintain
the spiritual origin of the universe, and worship the God whom
their opponents are so eager to dethrone. I must not, I suppose, include in my list Galileo, Kepler, Bacon, Newton,
Pascal, lest they should be objected to as not modern enough ;
though he must be strangely ignorant who should imagine that
they had not weighed and rejected the arguments for materialism which even now carry any real weight. But who will
question the attainments and authority of such men as Faraday,
Sir David Brewster, De Morgan, Herschell, Agassiz, Clerk-
Maxwell, Henry Smith, Balfour Stewart, Tait, Stokes, Rolleston,
Sir William Thompson?
  Nor for myself can I admit for a moment that the study of

we have to choose between their authority and
that of One whom even they themselves confess

science confers any special right to speak with authority on the
questions discussed in this essay.   For they are religious questions rather than scientific, and religious men of large intellect
and wide learning have surely as clear a right to be heard on
them as the men who have distinguished themselves as mathe-
maticians or physicists: such men, for example, as Bishops
Thirlwall and Lightfoot, Archbishop Thomson, Cardinal
Newman, Deans Stanley, Plumptre, Church, Canons Mozley,
Cook, Westcott, Barry, Drs. Salmon (of Dublin), Wace, Dale,
Tulloch, A. B. Davidson, Robertson Smith, Dykes, Maclaren,
with Maurice, Robertson, Lynch, and a hundred more who
might be named.

If we suspect both men of science and men of religion of bias,
conscious or unconscious, fit umpires might be found between
them in the great poets, statesmen, judges, artists, who have
done most to shape and rule our thoughts; or who by their
great natural gifts, wide and varied knowledge of men and
affairs, or their trained impartiality, would command our pro-
foundest respect : such men as Coleridge, Wordsworth, Tennyson, Browning, or Gladstone, Lords Selborne, Cairns, Coleridge,
or Carlyle, Ruskin, Kingsley, Holman Hunt.

Nothing would be easier than to add largely to all these lists
did time and space permit.   But the names cited will suffice to
call up many more, and to shew the young or credulous how
far it is from being true that the set of the best thought of the
day, in any province of human activity, is toward the dreary
and irrational materialism which a few able men, followed by
many who, save for their atheism, would in no way be distin-

to have been far better and wiser than themselves, entitled therefore to speak, at least on all
religious questions, with an authority transcend-
ing their own. And if we defer to what, in
various indirect ways, as well as by direct
confession, they themselves admit to be the
higher authority of the two, is there anything
unreasonable in that ?

(35) It may still further assist us in our
decision if we remember that on this point at
least, these representatives of modern and
advanced thought, really occupy the position
held two thousand years ago by the ignorant
Jewish bigots who rejected Christ and put Him
to death, hoping that by quenching the Light
of the world they might be left at peace in the
darkness which, for a well-known reason, they
preferred. For, like the Jewish Pharisees and

guished from their fellows, are so eager to promulgate. The
assumption that all logic and all ability are on the side of unbelief is an old weapon with its advocates. It has been used
again and again, but never with less excuse than now.

their scribes, our modern sceptics will not
believe unless they themselves see signs and
wonders. They reach their end indeed by a
different road to that along which the Jewish
bigots travelled ; but what of that if at last
we find them standing side by side ? The
Jews did not for a moment doubt that God
both could and did interfere with the operation
of natural forces and laws, or that He could
delegate that power to men ; but they would
not believe that He had delegated that power
to Jesus of Nazareth, since Jesus refused to
work in their presence the kind of miracle which
they demanded. Modern sceptics, on the other
hand, refuse either to believe that God ever did
exercise this power, or commission men to exercise it. But on what ground do they refuse ?
Simply on the ground that any such inter-
ference is contrary to their own experience and
to their reading of the experience of their
fellows. Before they will believe, they demand

that some miracle should be wrought in their presence, and submitted to their tests. In fine, they too must see signs and wonders or they will not believe. Like the Jews, they must have the very proof they demand before they will yield to the claim of the Son of Man.

How they will like the company into which they are thus brought, it is not for me to say ; but I do not see how they can deny that they are fairly brought into it, that they have brought themselves into it, and occupy the very ground on which the ignorant and furious bigots took their stand who rejected the testimony of God against themselves twenty centuries ago.

(36) And why should they maintain a position which its ancient defenders have rendered so suspicious ? How can they reasonably charge us with a sin against reason if we abandon it ? Only two hypotheses lie before us. The first is that which assumes that, because we see in

nature an impersonal order, there is nothing
more in it, an assumption which fails to account
even for the origin of matter and force; an
assumption which is obviously untrue, since
every man finds in nature at least one personality
—his own—and is compelled therefore to believe
in other personalities than his own. The second
hypothesis is that which assumes that, because
we are conscious of a living spirit within ourselves, the physical universe must be, if not the
body, at least the handiwork and garment of a
quickening Spirit, Almighty and Divine. This
second hypothesis not only accounts for the
origin of matter, energy, life, as well as for the
order of the universe, but it also alleges a cause
equal to all the effects we discover in the whole
round of being. It accounts for the existence
of intelligence and will, conscience and heart,
as well as for the existence of material atoms
and forces, and the laws by which they are
controlled. It is the larger and the more

natural, it is the only adequate, and therefore the only reasonable, hypothesis ; as indeed even sceptical men of science, leaders in the opposing school of thought, have admitted or affirmed. Thus, for example, John Stuart Mill, brushing aside the prepossessions and prejudices of a lifetime, has recorded his final and deliberate judgment,* that there is a large balance in favour of the probability of *creation by intelligence;* and Mr. Wallace, who shares with Darwin the honour of what many esteem the most fruitful discovery of modern science, confesses,† "It does not seem improbable that all force may be *will* force, and that the whole universe is not merely dependent upon, but actually *is*, the will of higher intelligences, or of one Supreme Intelligence."

In the face of these arguments and admissions, it is surely the height of unreason to charge us

* *Three Essays on Religion*, p. 174.
† *Contributions to the Theory of Natural Selection*, p. 368.

K

with unreasonableness if we give the preference
to that hypothesis which attributes both the
creation and the evolution of the universe to a
living and life-giving Spirit rather than to an
impersonal order or law which really accounts
for nothing, but has itself to be accounted for ;
if we take our stand by the side of the Centurion,
and conceive of the forces and laws of nature
as the obsequious servants of an all-seeing
Wisdom and an almighty Power.

(37) Nor can those who hold man to be the
sum and crown of things, the last and highest
product of natural forces and laws, and therefore
the glass in which the Maker of all things is
most clearly and fully reflected, reasonably condemn the belief in *Miracles* as irrational.   There
is a modern school of Theology as well as a
modern school of Science.   It is this modern
theology which modern science is bound to
meet.   To insist on the definitions and refute
the arguments of our fathers is no more fair

on their part than it would be fair on ours to run riot among, and hold them responsible for, the exploded scientific hypotheses of bygone ages. And we of the modern school do not contend, whatever our fathers may have done, that laws of nature must be suspended, abrogated, or reversed, whenever a miracle is wrought. We say that they must be *used* by an Intelligence infinitely higher than ours, and therefore an Intelligence which may well produce effects most strange and wonderful to us.* We point to the use which man has made of them in a thousand different ways—by his use of them changing the face of the whole world; and we argue that God may use them, for worthy ends, still more potently and admirably. In nature

* I do not, however, claim this as a purely modern discovery. Even Augustine must have had some glimpse of it when he wrote (*Contra Faustum*, xxvi. 3) : " God does nothing against nature. When we say that He does so, we mean that He does something against nature *as we know it*—in its familiar and ordinary way; but against the highest laws of nature He no more acts than He acts against Himself."

herself, we say, there are the materials by which
men are fed, healed, taught, served, and forces
by which, according at least to the fashionable
theory of the time, life is for ever being evolved
from lifelessness. Man has learned so to employ
these forces and materials as to compel them
to minister, in ways beyond the reach of un-
assisted nature, to his nourishment, his health,
his service. Why, then, we ask, should it be
deemed impossible for God so to use these
forces and laws, so to modify and control, so
to hasten and retard their operation, as to feed
and heal, to teach and serve men, and even to
give life to the dying or the dead in ways
beyond the measure of our minds? Is there
anything unreasonable in that?

(38) But if God holds all the forces and laws
of nature in the hollow of his hand, and can
use them for our good in ways unknown and
perhaps undiscoverable by us, not only do the
miracles of the Bible grow credible to us so

soon as we have evidence for them on which
we can depend ; but we also condemn ourselves
as unreasonable if we any longer doubt the
efficacy of *Prayer.* And of all the implications
of the Centurion's argument, this, to my mind,
is the most valuable and delightful, as it is also
the most obvious and direct. For what we
need most of all, as we stand hesitating and
bewildered among the perplexities of life and
conduct, is the conviction that we have a living
God who is still active, still working in and for
us, to whom we can appeal, in whom we can
trust, who will listen to us and answer us when
we call on Him for teaching, guidance, strength ;
and who can work miracles of grace for us even
though signs and wonders be no longer vouchsafed us. *This* is the conviction which sustained
the Centurion when he brought his prayer to
Christ, and which Christ Himself sanctioned
and confirmed by his admiration and approval
of the Centurion's faith. He might have had

a sign, a portent if he would but, strong in faith, he preferred a simple word, and no more doubted that that word would be obeyed than that his own word of command would be obeyed by those who served under him. Obviously he believed that the forces and laws of nature, animate and inanimate, were always doing the will of God, and that the Servant and Son of God, *without any signal or exceptional exertion of his power*, could heal his "boy," and would heal him if He felt that it was for the good of both servant and master that the "boy" should be healed. And this is the very conviction which we require in order to give depth and devotion, courage and hope, alike to our supplications and our lives. Why should we not cherish it and lean upon it? If God knows the natural forces and laws as we cannot know them, if He can and does use and control them for our good and for the general good; if, as we see, He does feed and heal, teach, guide, and sustain men by his wise use and administration of them, and that in ways past finding out ; why should not we ask of Him whatsoever things we need, or think the world needs, in the full assurance that He will listen to us, and either grant what it is really for our good to have, or teach us that his will is wiser and kinder than our own ? On this hypothesis, urged in this spirit, Prayer is not unreasonable, but most reasonable ; and we may, we ought to lay the *un*flattering but most cordial and invigorating unction to our souls, that, if we commit our way unto the Lord, He will give us the desire of our hearts.

(39) These, then, are the facts, and this is the argument which, as they should know, the sceptics and agnostics of the present day have to explain and refute before they can claim the attention of thoughtful and candid men. These facts and this argument are not stated here for

the first time. They have been stated again and again for the last thirty or forty years; and that by men of sufficient note; by such men, for example as Bersier of Paris, Godet of Neufchatel, Horace Bushnell, Newman Smyth, Phillips Brooks, Henry Ward Beecher, Theodore Munger, of America; by Thirlwall, Maurice, Erskine (of Linlathen), Kingsley, Stanley, Wace, Abbott, Lynch, Dale, Edward White, Martineau, and many more, in England. In short, they are the common property of that broader and more advanced school of thought in the Christian world which answers most nearly to the Darwinian school in the scientific world; though, for the special form in which they appear in this Essay, I am mainly indebted to Smyth's *Old Faiths in New Light* (in Chapter I.), to Godet's *Lectures in Defence of the Christian Faith* (in Chapter II.), and to an essay on *Prayer* in the *Expositor* for 1877 (in Chapter III.). And I think we may fairly challenge a reply to it, precisely

because it is not the product of a single mind,
but the common property of a large and growing
school of thought. As yet, however, I have not
met with a single serious attempt to answer it;
nor, indeed, with any serious attempt to under-
stand how the Bible reads, to those who believe
in it, in the light of the new scholarship and
exegesis. Our modern sceptics, at least on the
scientific side, so far as they condescend to argue
with us, are content to ignore the last and most
generous reading, and to carry themselves as
though the Roman or the Puritan, the Sacerdotal
or the Calvinistic interpretation of the Biblical
documents were all they had to meet; which
is about as fair as if *we* should content ourselves
with refuting the objections to the Christian
Faith raised by the sceptics of the pre-Dar-
winian, or even of the pre-Keplerian and pre-
Newtonian age, before Science had learned to
utter "that sweet word" Evolution—a feat of
which it is now so proud that it grows angry

should one venture to hint that it may some day learn to pronounce a still larger and nobler word. Should, however, any man of science undertake to reply to this argument, we can promise him that many will listen to him with the most profound and eager interest, and will honestly confess the force of his argument at any point at which they may find themselves unable to meet it. And, till then, we who accept the new theology can afford to take very calmly the charge of a bigoted insensibility to reason so often alleged against us by votaries of the new science.

Indeed it may and ought to be said, even in the interest of science itself, that the charge of bigotry comes with an ill grace from the lips of men who kindle into an Athanasian ire against all who do not instantly accept as true what they themselves must acknowledge to be an unverified, though most probable, hypothesis. Bigotry, alas, is confined to no school of thought,

though it is never so out of place as in the
school of Christ. It is the offspring of ignorance
and ill-will ; and is, it may be feared, quite as
commonly found among those who profess to
know as among these who profess to believe.
For while it would be easy to name many a
defender of the Faith who has honestly weighed
the latest hypothesis of science, and frankly
accepted its "discoveries," it would not be so
easy to name sceptical men of science who have
earnestly studied the Bible for themselves, and
have shewn an equal desire to weigh what it
has to urge in its own behalf. And this, I think,
we may fairly say, that until they meet the
Christian argument in its best and most reasonable form, the form given to it by its most
enlightened advocates ; so long as they assume,
for instance, that the Book of Genesis puts
forward a scientific cosmogony obviously unten-
able, or that the Church still holds a miracle
to be an infraction of law, or that the New

Testament either demands belief in doctrines rather than a good life, or teaches men to neglect the duties of this world in order to secure bliss in the world to come, and so makes selfishness rather than love its prime motive, or that it condemns the vast majority of men to an endless torment,—they shirk the real difficulties of the problem, evade the best and most advanced statement of the Christian hypothesis, and, in fine, behave themselves as foolishly as would the theologian or divine who should refute the scientific hypothesis in vogue a century ago, and pass by the science of to-day.

APR 1 5 1915

THE END.

PRINTED BY WILLIAM CLOWES AND SONS, LIMITED,
LONDON AND BECCLES.

A LIST OF

KEGAN PAUL, TRENCH & CO.'S

PUBLICATIONS.

1, *Paternoster Square,*
London.

A LIST OF

KEGAN PAUL, TRENCH & CO.'S PUBLICATIONS.

CONTENTS.

GENERAL LITERATURE.

ADAMSON, H. T., B.D.—The Truth as it is in Jesus. Crown 8vo, 8*s.* 6*d.*

The Three Sevens. Crown 8vo, 5*s.* 6*d.*

The Millennium; or, the Mystery of God Finished. Crown 8vo, 6*s.*

A. K. H. B.—From a Quiet Place. A New Volume of Sermons. Crown 8vo, 5*s.*

ALLEN, Rev. R., M.A.—Abraham: his Life, Times, and Travels, 3800 years ago. With Map. Second Edition. Post 8vo, 6*s.*

ALLIES, T. W., M.A.—Per Crucem ad Lucem. The Result of a Life. 2 vols. Demy 8vo, 25*s.*

A Life's Decision. Crown 8vo, 7*s.* 6*d.*

AMOS, Professor Sheldon.—The History and Principles of the Civil Law of Rome. An aid to the Study of Scientific and Comparative Jurisprudence. Demy 8vo. 16*s.*

ANDERDON, Rev. W. H.—Fasti Apostolici; a Chronology of the Years between the Ascension of our Lord and the Martyrdom of SS. Peter and Paul. Second Edition. Crown 8vo, 2*s.* 6*d.*

Evenings with the Saints. Crown 8vo, 5*s.*

ARMSTRONG, Richard A., B.A.—Latter-Day Teachers. Six Lectures. Small crown 8vo, 2*s.* 6*d.*

AUBERTIN, J. J.—A Flight to Mexico. With Seven full-page Illustrations and a Railway Map of Mexico. Crown 8vo, 7s. 6d.

BADGER, George Percy, D.C.L.—An English-Arabic Lexicon. In which the equivalent for English Words and Idiomatic Sentences are rendered into literary and colloquial Arabic. Royal 4to, £9 9s.

BAGEHOT, Walter.—The English Constitution. Third Edition. Crown 8vo, 7s. 6d.

> Lombard Street. A Description of the Money Market. Eighth Edition. Crown 8vo, 7s. 6d.

> Some Articles on the Depreciation of Silver, and Topics connected with it. Demy 8vo, 5s.

BAGENAL, Philip H.—The American-Irish and their Influence on Irish Politics. Crown 8vo, 5s.

BAGOT, Alan, C.E.—Accidents in Mines: their Causes and Prevention. Crown 8vo, 6s.

> The Principles of Colliery Ventilation. Second Edition, greatly enlarged. Crown 8vo, 5s.

BAKER, Sir Sherston, Bart.—The Laws relating to Quarantine. Crown 8vo, 12s. 6d.

BALDWIN, Capt. J. H.—The Large and Small Game of Bengal and the North-Western Provinces of India. With 18 Illustrations. New and Cheaper Edition. Small 4to, 10s. 6d.

BALLIN, Ada S. and F. L.—A Hebrew Grammar. With Exercises selected from the Bible. Crown 8vo, 7s. 6d.

BARCLAY, Edgar.—Mountain Life in Algeria. With numerous Illustrations by Photogravure. Crown 4to, 16s.

BARLOW, James H.—The Ultimatum of Pessimism. An Ethical Study. Demy 8vo, 6s.

BARNES, William.—Outlines of Redecraft (Logic). With English Wording. Crown 8vo, 3s.

BAUR, Ferdinand, Dr. Ph.—A Philological Introduction to Greek and Latin for Students. Translated and adapted from the German, by C. KEGAN PAUL, M.A., and E. D. STONE, M.A. Third Edition. Crown 8vo, 6s.

BELLARS, Rev. W.—The Testimony of Conscience to the Truth and Divine Origin of the Christian Revelation. Burney Prize Essay. Small crown 8vo, 3s. 6d.

BELLINGHAM, Henry, M.P.—Social Aspects of Catholicism and Protestantism in their Civil Bearing upon Nations. Translated and adapted from the French of M. le BARON DE HAULLEVILLE. With a preface by His Eminence CARDINAL MANNING. Second and Cheaper Edition. Crown 8vo, 3s. 6d.

BELLINGHAM H. Belsches Graham.—Ups and Downs of Spanish Travel. Second Edition. Crown 8vo. 5*s.*

BENN, Alfred W.—The Greek Philosophers. 2 vols. Demy 8vo, 28*s.*

BENT, J. Theodore.—Genoa : How the Republic Rose and Fell. With 18 Illustrations. Demy 8vo, 18*s.*

BLOOMFIELD, The Lady.—Reminiscences of Court and Diplomatic Life. New and Cheaper Edition. With Frontispiece. Crown 8vo, 6*s.*

BLUNT, The Ven. Archdeacon.—The Divine Patriot, and other Sermons. Preached in Scarborough and in Cannes. New and Cheaper Edition. Crown 8vo, 4*s.* 6*d.*

BLUNT, Wilfred S.—The Future of Islam. Crown 8vo, 6*s.*

BONWICK, J., F.R.G.S.—Pyramid Facts and Fancies. Crown 8vo, 5*s.*

BOUVERIE-PUSEY, S. E. B.—Permanence and Evolution. An Inquiry into the Supposed Mutability of Animal Types. Crown 8vo, 5*s.*

BOWEN, H. C., M.A.—Studies in English. For the use of Modern Schools. Third Edition. Small crown 8vo, 1*s.* 6*d.*

English Grammar for Beginners. Fcap. 8vo, 1*s.*

BRADLEY, F. H.—The Principles of Logic. Demy 8vo, 16*s.*

BRIDGETT, Rev. T. E.—History of the Holy Eucharist in Great Britain. 2 vols. Demy 8vo, 18*s.*

BRODRICK, the Hon. G. C.—Political Studies. Demy 8vo, 14*s.*

BROOKE, Rev. S. A.—Life and Letters of the Late Rev. F. W. Robertson, M.A. Edited by.

    I. Uniform with Robertson's Sermons. 2 vols. With Steel Portrait. 7*s.* 6*d.*
    II. Library Edition. With Portrait. 8vo, 12*s.*
    III. A Popular Edition. In 1 vol., 8vo, 6*s.*

The Fight of Faith. Sermons preached on various occasions. Fifth Edition. Crown 8vo, 7*s.* 6*d.*

The Spirit of the Christian Life. New and Cheaper Edition. Crown 8vo, 5*s.*

Theology in the English Poets.—Cowper, Coleridge, Wordsworth, and Burns. Fifth and Cheaper Edition. Post 8vo, 5*s.*

Christ in Modern Life. Sixteenth and Cheaper Edition. Crown 8vo, 5*s.*

Sermons. First Series. Thirteenth and Cheaper Edition. Crown 8vo, 5*s.*

Sermons. Second Series. Sixth and Cheaper Edition. Crown 8vo, 5*s.*

BROWN, Rev. J. Baldwin, B.A.—The Higher Life. Its Reality, Experience, and Destiny. Fifth Edition. Crown 8vo, 5*s*.

Doctrine of Annihilation in the Light of the Gospel of Love. Five Discourses. Fourth Edition. Crown 8vo, 2*s*. 6*d*.

The Christian Policy of Life. A Book for Young Men of Business. Third Edition. Crown 8vo, 3*s*. 6*d*.

BROWN, S. Borton, B.A.—The Fire Baptism of all Flesh; or, the Coming Spiritual Crisis of the Dispensation. Crown 8vo, 6*s*.

BROWNBILL, John.—Principles of English Canon Law. Part I. General Introduction. Crown 8vo, 6*s*.

BROWNE, W. R.—The Inspiration of the New Testament. With a Preface by the Rev. J. P. NORRIS, D.D. Fcap. 8vo, 2*s*. 6*d*.

BURTON, Mrs. Richard.—The Inner Life of Syria, Palestine, and the Holy Land. Cheaper Edition in one volume. Large post 8vo. 7*s*. 6*d*.

BUSBECQ, Ogier Ghiselin de.—His Life and Letters. By CHARLES THORNTON FORSTER, M.A., and F. H. BLACKBURNE DANIELL, M.A. 2 vols. With Frontispieces. Demy 8vo, 24*s*.

CARPENTER, W. B., LL.D., M.D., F.R.S., etc.—The Principles of Mental Physiology. With their Applications to the Training and Discipline of the Mind, and the Study of its Morbid Conditions. Illustrated. Sixth Edition. 8vo, 12*s*.

CERVANTES.—The Ingenious Knight Don Quixote de la Mancha. A New Translation from the Originals of 1605 and 1608. By A. J. DUFFIELD. With Notes. 3 vols. Demy 8vo, 42*s*.

Journey to Parnassus. Spanish Text, with Translation into English Tercets, Preface, and Illustrative Notes, by JAMES Y. GIBSON. Crown 8vo, 12*s*.

CHEYNE, Rev. T. K.—The Prophecies of Isaiah. Translated with Critical Notes and Dissertations. 2 vols. Second Edition. Demy 8vo, 25*s*.

CLAIRAUT.—Elements of Geometry. Translated by Dr. KAINES. With 145 Figures. Crown 8vo, 4*s*. 6*d*.

CLAYDEN, P. W.—England under Lord Beaconsfield. The Political History of the Last Six Years, from the end of 1873 to the beginning of 1880. Second Edition, with Index and continuation to March, 1880. Demy 8vo, 16*s*.

Samuel Sharpe. Egyptologist and Translator of the Bible. Crown 8vo, 6*s*.

CLIFFORD, Samuel.—What Think Ye of Christ? Crown 8vo. 6*s*.

CLODD, Edward, F.R.A.S.—The Childhood of the World: a Simple Account of Man in Early Times. Seventh Edition. Crown 8vo, 3*s*.
A Special Edition for Schools. 1*s*.

CLODD, Edward, F.R.A.S.—continued.

The Childhood of Religions. Including a Simple Account of the Birth and Growth of Myths and Legends. Eighth Thousand. Crown 8vo, 5*s.*
A Special Edition for Schools. 1*s.* 6*d.*

Jesus of Nazareth. With a brief sketch of Jewish History to the Time of His Birth. Small crown 8vo, 6*s.*

COGHLAN, J. Cole, D.D.—The Modern Pharisee and other Sermons. Edited by the Very Rev. H. H. DICKINSON, D.D., Dean of Chapel Royal, Dublin. New and Cheaper Edition. Crown 8vo, 7*s.* 6*d.*

COLERIDGE, Sara.—Memoir and Letters of Sara Coleridge. Edited by her Daughter. With Index. Cheap Edition. With Portrait. 7*s.* 6*d.*

Collects Exemplified. Being Illustrations from the Old and New Testaments of the Collects for the Sundays after Trinity. By the Author of " A Commentary on the Epistles and Gospels." Edited by the Rev. JOSEPH JACKSON. Crown 8vo, 5*s.*

CONNELL, A. K.—Discontent and Danger in India. Small crown 8vo, 3*s.* 6*d.*

The Economic Revolution of India. Crown 8vo, 5*s.*

CORY, William.—A Guide to Modern English History. Part I. —MDCCCXV.-MDCCCXXX. Demy 8vo, 9*s.* Part II.— MDCCCXXX.-MDCCCXXXV., 15*s.*

COTTERILL, H. B.—An Introduction to the Study of Poetry. Crown 8vo, 7*s.* 6*d.*

COX, Rev. Sir George W., M.A., Bart.—A History of Greece from the Earliest Period to the end of the Persian War. New Edition. 2 vols. Demy 8vo, 36*s.*

The Mythology of the Aryan Nations. New Edition. Demy 8vo, 16*s.*

Tales of Ancient Greece. New Edition. Small crown 8vo, 6*s.*

A Manual of Mythology in the form of Question and Answer. New Edition. Fcap. 8vo, 3*s.*

An Introduction to the Science of Comparative Mythology and Folk-Lore. Second Edition. Crown 8vo. 7*s.* 6*d.*

COX, Rev. Sir G. W., M.A., Bart., and JONES, Eustace Hinton.— Popular Romances of the Middle Ages. Second Edition, in 1 vol. Crown 8vo, 6*s.*

COX, Rev. Samuel, D.D.—Salvator Mundi ; or, Is Christ the Saviour of all Men ? Eighth Edition. Crown 8vo, 5*s.*

The Genesis of Evil, and other Sermons, mainly expository. Third Edition. Crown 8vo, 6*s.*

COX, Rev. Samuel, D.D.—continued.

A Commentary on the Book of Job. With a Translation. Demy 8vo, 15*s*.

The Larger Hope. A Sequel to "Salvator Mundi." 16mo, 1*s*.

*CRAVEN, Mrs.—*A Year's Meditations. Crown 8vo, 6*s*.

*CRAWFURD, Oswald.—*Portugal, Old and New. With Illustrations and Maps. New and Cheaper Edition. Crown 8vo, 6*s*.

*CROZIER, John Beattie, M.B.—*The Religion of the Future. Crown 8vo, 6*s*.

Cyclopædia of Common Things. Edited by the Rev. Sir GEORGE W. Cox, Bart., M.A. With 500 Illustrations. Third Edition. Large post 8vo, 7*s*. 6*d*.

*DAVIDSON, Rev. Samuel, D.D., LL.D.—*Canon of the Bible : Its Formation, History, and Fluctuations. Third and Revised Edition. Small crown 8vo, 5*s*.

The Doctrine of Last Things contained in the New Testament compared with the Notions of the Jews and the Statements of Church Creeds. Small crown 8vo, 3*s*. 6*d*.

*DAVIDSON, Thomas.—*The Parthenon Frieze, and other Essays. Crown 8vo, 6*s*.

DAWSON, Geo., M.A. Prayers, with a Discourse on Prayer. Edited by his Wife. Eighth Edition. Crown 8vo, 6*s*.

Sermons on Disputed Points and Special Occasions. Edited by his Wife. Fourth Edition. Crown 8vo, 6*s*.

Sermons on Daily Life and Duty. Edited by his Wife. Fourth Edition. Crown 8vo, 6*s*.

The Authentic Gospel. A New Volume of Sermons. Edited by GEORGE ST. CLAIR. Third Edition. Crown 8vo, 6*s*.

Three Books of God : Nature, History, and Scripture. Sermons edited by GEORGE ST. CLAIR. Crown 8vo, 6*s*.

*DE JONCOURT, Madame Marie.—*Wholesome Cookery. Crown 8vo, 3*s*. 6*d*.

*DE LONG, Lieut. Com. G. W.—*The Voyage of the Jeannette. The Ship and Ice Journals of. Edited by his Wife, EMMA DE LONG. With Portraits, Maps, and many Illustrations on wood and stone. 2 vols. Demy 8vo. 36*s*.

*DESPREZ, Phillip S., B.D.—*Daniel and John ; or, the Apocalypse of the Old and that of the New Testament. Demy 8vo, 12*s*.

*DOWDEN, Edward, LL.D.—*Shakspere : a Critical Study of his Mind and Art. Sixth Edition. Post 8vo, 12*s*.

Studies in Literature, 1789-1877. Second and Cheaper Edition. Large post 8vo, 6*s*.

DUFFIELD, A. J.—Don Quixote: his Critics and Commentators. With a brief account of the minor works of MIGUEL DE CERVANTES SAAVEDRA, and a statement of the aim and end of the greatest of them all. A handy book for general readers. Crown 8vo, 3*s.* 6*d.*

DU MONCEL, Count.—The Telephone, the Microphone, and the Phonograph. With 74 Illustrations. Second Edition. Small crown 8vo, 5*s.*

EDGEWORTH, F. Y.—Mathematical Psychics. An Essay on the Application of Mathematics to Social Science. Demy 8vo, 7*s.* 6*d.*

Educational Code of the Prussian Nation, in its Present Form. In accordance with the Decisions of the Common Provincial Law, and with those of Recent Legislation. Crown 8vo, 2*s.* 6*d.*

Education Library. Edited by PHILIP MAGNUS :—

An Introduction to the History of Educational Theories. By OSCAR BROWNING, M.A. Second Edition. 3*s.* 6*d.*

Old Greek Education. By the Rev. Prof. MAHAFFY, M.A. 3*s.* 6*d.*

School Management. Including a general view of the work of Education, Organization and Discipline. By JOSEPH LANDON. Second Edition. 6*s.*

Eighteenth Century Essays. Selected and Edited by AUSTIN DOBSON. With a Miniature Frontispiece by R. Caldecott. Parchment Library Edition, 6*s.* ; vellum, 7*s.* 6*d.*

ELSDALE, Henry.—Studies in Tennyson's Idylls. Crown 8vo, 5*s.*

ELYOT, Sir Thomas.—The Boke named the Gouernour. Edited from the First Edition of 1531 by HENRY HERBERT STEPHEN CROFT, M.A., Barrister-at-Law. With Portraits of Sir Thomas and Lady Elyot, copied by permission of her Majesty from Holbein's Original Drawings at Windsor Castle. 2 vols. Fcap. 4to, 50*s.*

Enoch the Prophet. The Book of. Archbishop LAURENCE'S Translation, with an Introduction by the Author of "The Evolution of Christianity." Crown 8vo, 5*s.*

Eranus. A Collection of Exercises in the Alcaic and Sapphic Metres. Edited by F. W. CORNISH, Assistant Master at Eton. Crown 8vo, 2*s.*

EVANS, Mark.—The Story of Our Father's Love, told to Children. Sixth and Cheaper Edition. With Four Illustrations. Fcap. 8vo, 1*s.* 6*d.*

EVANS, Mark—continued.

A Book of Common Prayer and Worship for Household Use, compiled exclusively from the Holy Scriptures. Second Edition. Fcap. 8vo, 1s.

The Gospel of Home Life. Crown 8vo, 4s. 6d.

The King's Story-Book. In Three Parts. Fcap. 8vo, 1s. 6d. each.

⁎⁎ Parts I. and II. with Eight Illustrations and Two Picture Maps, now ready.

"Fan Kwae" at Canton before Treaty Days 1825-1844. By an old Resident. With Frontispiece. Crown 8vo, 5s.

FLECKER, Rev. Eliezer.—Scripture Onomatology. Being Critical Notes on the Septuagint and other versions. Crown 8vo, 3s. 6d.

FLOREDICE, W. H.—A Month among the Mere Irish. Small crown 8vo, 5s.

GARDINER, Samuel R., and J. BASS MULLINGER, M.A.— Introduction to the Study of English History. Large Crown 8vo, 9s.

GARDNER, Dorsey.—Quatre Bras, Ligny, and Waterloo. A Narrative of the Campaign in Belgium, 1815. With Maps and Plans. Demy 8vo, 16s.

Genesis in Advance of Present Science. A Critical Investigation of Chapters I.-IX. By a Septuagenarian Beneficed Presbyter. Demy 8vo. 10s. 6d.

GENNA, E. — Irresponsible Philanthropists. Being some Chapters on the Employment of Gentlewomen. Small crown 8vo, 2s. 6d.

GEORGE, Henry.—Progress and Poverty : An Inquiry into the Causes of Industrial Depressions, and of Increase of Want with Increase of Wealth. The Remedy. Second Edition. Post 8vo, 7s. 6d. Also a Cheap Edition. Limp cloth, 1s. 6d. Paper covers, 1s.

GIBSON, James Y.—Journey to Parnassus. Composed by MIGUEL DE CERVANTES SAAVEDRA. Spanish Text, with Translation into English Tercets, Preface, and Illustrative Notes, by. Crown 8vo, 12s.

Glossary of Terms and Phrases. Edited by the Rev. H. PERCY SMITH and others. Medium 8vo, 12s.

GLOVER, F., M.A.—Exempla Latina. A First Construing Book, with Short Notes, Lexicon, and an Introduction to the Analysis of Sentences. Fcap. 8vo, 2s.

GOLDSMID, Sir Francis Henry, Bart., Q.C., M.P.—Memoir of. With Portrait. Second Edition, Revised. Crown 8vo, 6s.

GOODENOUGH, Commodore J. G.—Memoir of, with Extracts from his Letters and Journals. Edited by his Widow. With Steel Engraved Portrait. Square 8vo, 5*s*.

** Also a Library Edition with Maps, Woodcuts, and Steel Engraved Portrait. Square post 8vo, 14*s*.

GOSSE, Edmund W.—Studies in the Literature of Northern Europe. With a Frontispiece designed and etched by Alma Tadema. New and Cheaper Edition. Large crown 8vo, 6*s*.

Seventeenth Century Studies. A Contribution to the History of English Poetry. Demy 8vo, 10*s*. 6*d*.

GOULD, Rev. S. Baring, M.A.—Germany, Present and Past. New and Cheaper Edition. Large crown 8vo, 7*s*. 6*d*.

GOWAN, Major Walter E.—A. Ivanoff's Russian Grammar. (16th Edition.) Translated, enlarged, and arranged for use of Students of the Russian Language. Demy 8vo, 6*s*.

GOWER, Lord Ronald. My Reminiscences. Second Edition. 2 vols. With Frontispieces. Demy 8vo, 30*s*.

GRAHAM, William, M.A.—The Creed of Science, Religious, Moral, and Social. Demy 8vo, 6*s*.

GRIFFITH, Thomas, A.M.—The Gospel of the Divine Life: a Study of the Fourth Evangelist. Demy 8vo, 14*s*.

GRIMLEY, Rev. H. N., M.A.—Tremadoc Sermons, chiefly on the Spiritual Body, the Unseen World, and the Divine Humanity. Third Edition. Crown 8vo, 6*s*.

HAECKEL, Prof. Ernst.—The History of Creation. Translation revised by Professor E. RAY LANKESTER, M.A., F.R.S. With Coloured Plates and Genealogical Trees of the various groups of both Plants and Animals. 2 vols. Third Edition. Post 8vo, 32*s*.

The History of the Evolution of Man. With numerous Illustrations. 2 vols. Post 8vo, 32*s*.

A Visit to Ceylon. Post 8vo, 7*s*. 6*d*.

Freedom in Science and Teaching. With a Prefatory Note by T. H. HUXLEY, F.R.S. Crown 8vo, 5*s*.

HALF-CROWN SERIES :—

A Lost Love. By ANNA C. OGLE [Ashford Owen].

Sister Dora : a Biography. By MARGARET LONSDALE.

True Words for Brave Men : a Book for Soldiers and Sailors. By the late CHARLES KINGSLEY.

An Inland Voyage. By R. L. STEVENSON.

Travels with a Donkey. By R. L. STEVENSON.

HALF-CROWN SERIES—*continued.*

Notes of Travel : being Extracts from the Journals of Count VON MOLTKE.

English Sonnets. Collected and Arranged by J. DENNIS.

London Lyrics. By F. LOCKER.

Home Songs for Quiet Hours. By the Rev. Canon R. H. BAYNES.

HAWEIS, Rev. H. R., M.A.—Current Coin. Materialism—The Devil—Crime—Drunkenness—Pauperism—Emotion—Recreation —The Sabbath. Fifth and Cheaper Edition. Crown 8vo, 5s.

Arrows in the Air. Fifth and Cheaper Edition. Crown 8vo, 5s.

Speech in Season. Fifth and Cheaper Edition. Crown 8vo, 5s.

Thoughts for the Times. Thirteenth and Cheaper Edition. Crown 8vo, 5s.

Unsectarian Family Prayers. New and Cheaper Edition. Fcap. 8vo, 1s. 6d.

HAWKINS, Edwards Comerford.—Spirit and Form. Sermons preached in the Parish Church of Leatherhead. Crown 8vo, 6s.

HAWTHORNE, Nathaniel.—Works. Complete in Twelve Volumes. Large post 8vo, 7s. 6d. each volume.

VOL. I. TWICE-TOLD TALES.
II. MOSSES FROM AN OLD MANSE.
III. THE HOUSE OF THE SEVEN GABLES, AND THE SNOW IMAGE.
IV. THE WONDERBOOK, TANGLEWOOD TALES, AND GRANDFATHER'S CHAIR.
V. THE SCARLET LETTER, AND THE BLITHEDALE ROMANCE.
VI. THE MARBLE FAUN. [Transformation.]
VII. } OUR OLD HOME, AND ENGLISH NOTE-BOOKS.
VIII. }
IX. AMERICAN NOTE-BOOKS.
X. FRENCH AND ITALIAN NOTE-BOOKS.
XI. SEPTIMIUS FELTON, THE DOLLIVER ROMANCE, FANSHAWE, AND, IN AN APPENDIX, THE ANCESTRAL FOOTSTEP.
XII. TALES AND ESSAYS, AND OTHER PAPERS, WITH A BIOGRAPHICAL SKETCH OF HAWTHORNE.

HAYES, A. H., Junr.—New Colorado, and the Santa Fé Trail. With Map and 60 Illustrations. Crown 8vo, 9s.

HENNESSY, Sir John Pope.—Ralegh in Ireland. With his Letters on Irish Affairs and some Contemporary Documents. Large crown 8vo, printed on hand-made paper, parchment, 10s. 6d.

HENRY, Philip.—Diaries and Letters of. Edited by MATTHEW HENRY LEE, M.A. Large crown 8vo, 7s. 6d.

HIDE, Albert.—The Age to Come. Small crown 8vo, 2s. 6d.

HIME, Major H. W. L., R.A.—**Wagnerism : A Protest.** Crown 8vo, 2s. 6d.

HINTON, J.—**Life and Letters.** Edited by ELLICE HOPKINS, with an Introduction by Sir W. W. GULL, Bart., and Portrait engraved on Steel by C. H. Jeens. Fourth Edition. Crown 8vo, 8s. 6d.

The Mystery of Pain. New Edition. Fcap. 8vo, 1s.

HOLTHAM, E. G.—**Eight Years in Japan, 1873-1881.** Work, Travel, and Recreation. With three maps. Large crown 8vo, 9s.

HOOPER, Mary.—**Little Dinners : How to Serve them with Elegance and Economy.** Seventeenth Edition. Crown 8vo, 2s. 6d.

Cookery for Invalids, Persons of Delicate Digestion, and Children. Third Edition. Crown 8vo, 2s. 6d.

Every-Day Meals. Being Economical and Wholesome Recipes for Breakfast, Luncheon, and Supper. Fifth Edition. Crown 8vo, 2s. 6d.

HOPKINS, Ellice.—**Life and Letters of James Hinton,** with an Introduction by Sir W. W. GULL, Bart., and Portrait engraved on Steel by C. H. Jeens. Fourth Edition. Crown 8vo, 8s. 6d.

Work amongst Working Men. Fourth edition. Crown 8vo, 3s. 6d.

HOSPITALIER, E.—**The Modern Applications of Electricity.** Translated and Enlarged by JULIUS MAIER, Ph.D. 2 vols. With numerous Illustrations. Demy 8vo, 12s. 6d. each volume.
VOL. I.—Electric Generators, Electric Light.
VOL. II.—Telephone : Various Applications : Electrical Transmission of Energy.

Household Readings on Prophecy. By a Layman. Small crown 8vo, 3s. 6d.

HUGHES, Henry.—**The Redemption of the World.** Crown 8vo, 3s. 6d.

HUNTINGFORD, Rev. E., D.C.L.—**The Apocalypse.** With a Commentary and Introductory Essay. Demy 8vo, 9s.

HUTTON, Arthur, M.A.—**The Anglican Ministry :** Its Nature and Value in relation to the Catholic Priesthood. With a Preface by His Eminence CARDINAL NEWMAN. Demy 8vo, 14s.

HUTTON, Rev. C. F.—**Unconscious Testimony ;** or, the Silent Witness of the Hebrew to the Truth of the Historical Scriptures. Crown 8vo, 2s. 6d.

IM THURN, Everard F.—**Among the Indians of British Guiana.** Being Sketches, chiefly anthropologic, from the Interior of British Guiana. With numerous Illustrations. Demy 8vo.

JENKINS, E., and RAYMOND, J.—The Architect's Legal Handbook. Third Edition, Revised. Crown 8vo, 6s.

JENKINS, Rev. R. C., M.A.—The Privilege of Peter, and the Claims of the Roman Church confronted with the Scriptures, the Councils, and the Testimony of the Popes themselves. Fcap. 8vo, 3s. 6d.

JERVIS, Rev. W. Henley.— The Gallican Church and the Revolution. A Sequel to the History of the Church of France, from the Concordat of Bologna to the Revolution. Demy 8vo, 18s.

JOEL, L.—A Consul's Manual and Shipowner's and Shipmaster's Practical Guide in their Transactions Abroad. With Definitions of Nautical, Mercantile, and Legal Terms; a Glossary of Mercantile Terms in English, French, German, Italian, and Spanish; Tables of the Money, Weights, and Measures of the Principal Commercial Nations and their Equivalents in British Standards; and Forms of Consular and Notarial Acts. Demy 8vo, 12s.

JOHNSTONE, C. F., M.A.—Historical Abstracts : being Outlines of the History of some of the less known States of Europe. Crown 8vo, 7s. 6d.

JOLLY, William, F.R.S.E., etc.—The Life of John Duncan, Scotch Weaver and Botanist. With Sketches of his Friends and Notices of his Times. Second Edition. Large crown 8vo, with etched portrait, 9s.

JONES, C. A.—The Foreign Freaks of Five Friends. With 30 Illustrations. Crown 8vo, 6s.

JOYCE, P. W., LL.D., etc.—Old Celtic Romances. Translated from the Gaelic. Crown 8vo, 7s. 6d.

JOYNES, J. L.—The Adventures of a Tourist in Ireland. Second edition. Small crown 8vo, 2s. 6d.

KAUFMANN, Rev. M., B.A.—Socialism : its Nature, its Dangers, and its Remedies considered. Crown 8vo, 7s. 6d.

Utopias ; or, Schemes of Social Improvement, from Sir Thomas More to Karl Marx. Crown 8vo, 5s.

KAY, Joseph.—Free Trade in Land. Edited by his Widow. With Preface by the Right Hon. JOHN BRIGHT, M.P. Sixth Edition. Crown 8vo, 5s.

KEMPIS, Thomas à.—Of the Imitation of Christ. Parchment Library Edition, 6s. ; or vellum, 7s. 6d. The Red Line Edition, fcap. 8vo, red edges, 2s. 6d. The Cabinet Edition, small 8vo, cloth limp, 1s. ; cloth boards, red edges, 1s. 6d. The Miniature Edition, red edges, 32mo, 1s.

⁎⁎⁎ All the above Editions may be had in various extra bindings.

KENT, C.—Corona Catholica ad Petri successoris Pedes Oblata. De Summi Pontificis Leonis XIII. Assumptione Epigramma. In Quinquaginta Linguis. Fcap. 4to, 15s.

KETTLEWELL, Rev. S.—Thomas à Kempis and the Brothers of Common Life. 2 vols. With Frontispieces. Demy 8vo, 30*s.*

KIDD, Joseph, M.D.—The Laws of Therapeutics ; or, the Science and Art of Medicine. Second Edition. Crown 8vo, 6*s.*

KINGSFORD, Anna, M.D.—The Perfect Way in Diet. A Treatise advocating a Return to the Natural and Ancient Food of our Race. Small crown 8vo, 2*s.*

KINGSLEY, Charles, M.A.—Letters and Memories of his Life. Edited by his Wife. With two Steel Engraved Portraits, and Vignettes on Wood. Thirteenth Cabinet Edition. 2 vols. Crown 8vo, 12*s.*

** Also a New and Condensed Edition, in one volume. With Portrait. Crown 8vo, 6*s.*

All Saints' Day, and other Sermons. Also a new and condensed Edition in one volume, with Portrait. Crown 8vo, 6*s.* Edited by the Rev. W. HARRISON. Third Edition. Crown 8vo, 7*s.* 6*d.*

True Words for Brave Men. A Book for Soldiers' and Sailors' Libraries. Tenth Edition. Crown 8vo, 2*s.* 6*d.*

KNOX, Alexander A.—The New Playground ; or, Wanderings in Algeria. New and cheaper edition. Large crown 8vo, 6*s.*

LANDON Joseph.—School Management ; Including a General View of the Work of Education, Organization, and Discipline. Second Edition. Crown 8vo, 6*s.*

LAURIE, S. S.—The Training of Teachers, and other Educational Papers. Crown 8vo, 7*s.* 6*d.*

LEE, Rev. F. G., D.C.L.—The Other World ; or, Glimpses of the Supernatural. 2 vols. A New Edition. Crown 8vo, 15*s.*

Letters from a Young Emigrant in Manitoba. Second Edition. Small crown 8vo, 3*s.* 6*d.*

LEWIS, Edward Dillon.—A Draft Code of Criminal Law and Procedure. Demy 8vo, 21*s.*

LILLIE, Arthur, M.R.A.S.—The Popular Life of Buddha. Containing an Answer to the Hibbert Lectures of 1881. With Illustrations. Crown 8vo, 6*s.*

LINDSAY, W. Lauder, M.D.—Mind in the Lower Animals in Health and Disease. 2 vols. Demy 8vo, 32*s.*

Vol. I.—Mind in Health. Vol. II.—Mind in Disease.

LLOYD, Walter.—The Hope of the World : An Essay on Universal Redemption. Crown 8vo, 5*s.*

LONSDALE, Margaret.—Sister Dora : a Biography. With Portrait. Twenty-fifth Edition. Crown 8vo, 2*s.* 6*d.*

LOWDER, Charles.—A Biography. By the Author of " St. Teresa." New and Cheaper Edition. Crown 8vo. With Portrait. 3*s.* 6*d.*

LYTTON, Edward Bulwer, Lord.—Life, Letters and Literary Remains. By his Son, The EARL OF LYTTON. With Portraits, Illustrations and Facsimiles. Demy 8vo.
[Vols. I. and II. just ready.

MACHIAVELLI, Niccolò.—Discourses on the First Decade of Titus Livius. Translated from the Italian by NINIAN HILL THOMSON, M.A. Large crown 8vo, 12*s.*

The Prince. Translated from the Italian by N. H. T. Small crown 8vo, printed on hand-made paper, bevelled boards, 6*s.*

MACKENZIE, Alexander.—How India is Governed. Being an Account of England's Work in India. Small crown 8vo, 2*s.*

MACNAUGHT, Rev. John.—Cœna Domini : An Essay on the Lord's Supper, its Primitive Institution, Apostolic Uses, and Subsequent History. Demy 8vo, 14*s.*

MACWALTER, Rev. G. S.—Life of Antonis Rosmini Serbati (Founder of the Institute of Charity). 2 vols. Demy 8vo.
[Vol. I. now ready, price 12*s.*

MAGNUS, Mrs.—About the Jews since Bible Times. From the Babylonian Exile till the English Exodus. Small crown 8vo, 6*s.*

MAIR, R. S., M.D., F.R.C.S.E.—The Medical Guide for Anglo-Indians. Being a Compendium of Advice to Europeans in India, relating to the Preservation and Regulation of Health. With a Supplement on the Management of Children in India. Second Edition. Crown 8vo, limp cloth, 3*s.* 6*d.*

MALDEN, Henry Elliot.—Vienna, 1683. The History and Consequences of the Defeat of the Turks before Vienna, September 12th, 1683, by John Sobieski, King of Poland, and Charles Leopold, Duke of Lorraine. Crown 8vo, 4*s.* 6*d.*

Many Voices. A volume of Extracts from the Religious Writers of Christendom from the First to the Sixteenth Century. With Biographical Sketches. Crown 8vo, cloth extra, red edges, 6*s.*

MARKHAM, Capt. Albert Hastings, R.N.—The Great Frozen Sea : A Personal Narrative of the Voyage of the *Alert* during the Arctic Expedition of 1875-6. With 6 Full-page Illustrations, 2 Maps, and 27 Woodcuts. Sixth and Cheaper Edition. Crown 8vo, 6*s.*

A Polar Reconnaissance : being the Voyage of the *Isbjörn* to Novaya Zemlya in 1879. With 10 Illustrations. Demy 8vo, 16*s.*

Marriage and Maternity ; or, Scripture Wives and Mothers. Small crown 8vo, 4*s.* 6*d.*

MARTINEAU, Gertrude.—Outline Lessons on Morals. Small crown 8vo, 3*s.* 6*d.*

MAUDSLEY, H., M.D.—Body and Will. Being an Essay concerning Will, in its Metaphysical, Physiological, and Pathological Aspects. 8vo, 12*s.*

McGRATH, Terence.—Pictures from Ireland. New and Cheaper Edition. Crown 8vo, 2*s.*

MEREDITH, M.A.—Theotokos, the Example for Woman. Dedicated, by permission, to Lady Agnes Wood. Revised by the Venerable Archdeacon DENISON. 32mo, limp cloth, 1*s.* 6*d.*

MILLER, Edward.—The History and Doctrines of Irvingism ; or, the so-called Catholic and Apostolic Church. 2 vols. Large post 8vo, 25*s.*

   The Church in Relation to the State. Large crown 8vo, 7*s.* 6*d.*

MINCHIN, J. G.—Bulgaria since the War : Notes of a Tour in the Autumn of 1879. Small crown 8vo, 3*s.* 6*d.*

MITFORD, Bertram.—Through the Zulu Country. Its Battle-fields and its People. With five Illustrations. Demy 8vo, 14*s.*

MIVART, St. George.—Nature and Thought : An Introduction to a Natural Philosophy. Demy 8vo, 10*s.* 6*d.*

MOCKLER, E.—A Grammar of the Baloochee Language, as it is spoken in Makran (Ancient Gedrosia), in the Persia-Arabic and Roman characters. Fcap. 8vo, 5*s.*

MOLESWORTH, Rev. W. Nassau, M.A.—History of the Church of England from 1660. Large crown 8vo, 7*s.* 6*d.*

MORELL, J. R.—Euclid Simplified in Method and Language. Being a Manual of Geometry. Compiled from the most important French Works, approved by the University of Paris and the Minister of Public Instruction. Fcap. 8vo, 2*s.* 6*d.*

MORSE, E. S., Ph.D.—First Book of Zoology. With numerous Illustrations. New and Cheaper Edition. Crown 8vo, 2*s.* 6*d.*

MURPHY, John Nicholas.—The Chair of Peter ; or, the Papacy considered in its Institution, Development, and Organization, and in the Benefits which for over Eighteen Centuries it has conferred on Mankind. Demy 8vo, 18*s.*

NELSON, J. H., M.A.—A Prospectus of the Scientific Study of the Hindû Law. Demy 8vo, 9*s.*

NEWMAN, J. H., D.D.—Characteristics from the Writings of. Being Selections from his various Works. Arranged with the Author's personal Approval. Sixth Edition. With Portrait. Crown 8vo, 6*s.*

   ₊₊* A Portrait of Cardinal Newman, mounted for framing, can be had, 2*s.* 6*d.*

NEWMAN, Francis William.—Essays on Diet. Small crown 8vo, cloth limp, 2*s.*

New Werther. By LOKI. Small crown 8vo, 2*s.* 6*d.*

NICHOLSON, Edward Byron.—The Gospel according to the Hebrews. Its Fragments Translated and Annotated with a Critical Analysis of the External and Internal Evidence relating to it. Demy 8vo, 9s. 6d.

A New Commentary on the Gospel according to Matthew. Demy 8vo, 12s.

NICOLS, Arthur, F.G.S., F.R.G.S.—Chapters from the Physical History of the Earth: an Introduction to Geology and Palæontology. With numerous Illustrations. Crown 8vo, 5s.

NOPS, Marianne.—Class Lessons on Euclid. Part I. containing the First two Books of the Elements. Crown 8vo, 2s. 6d.

Notes on St. Paul's Epistle to the Galatians. For Readers of the Authorized Version or the Original Greek. Demy 8vo, 2s. 6d.

Nuces : EXERCISES ON THE SYNTAX OF THE PUBLIC SCHOOL LATIN PRIMER. New Edition in Three Parts. Crown 8vo, each 1s.
₊ The Three Parts can also be had bound together, 3s.

OATES, Frank, F.R.G.S.—Matabele Land and the Victoria Falls. A Naturalist's Wanderings in the Interior of South Africa. Edited by C. G. OATES, B.A. With numerous Illustrations and 4 Maps. Demy 8vo, 21s.

OGLE, W., M.D., F.R.C.P.—Aristotle on the Parts of Animals. Translated, with Introduction and Notes. Royal 8vo, 12s. 6d.

Oken Lorenz, Life of. By ALEXANDER ECKER. With Explanatory Notes, Selections from Oken's Correspondence, and Portrait of the Professor. From the German by ALFRED TULK. Crown 8vo, 6s.

O'MEARA, Kathleen.—Frederic Ozanam, Professor of the Sorbonne : His Life and Work. Second Edition. Crown 8vo, 7s. 6d.

Henri Perreyve and his Counsels to the Sick. Small crown 8vo, 5s.

OSBORNE, Rev. W. A.—The Revised Version of the New Testament. A Critical Commentary, with Notes upon the Text. Crown 8vo, 5s.

OTTLEY, H. Bickersteth.—The Great Dilemma. Christ His Own Witness or His Own Accuser. Six Lectures. Second Edition. Crown 8vo, 3s. 6d.

Our Public Schools—Eton, Harrow, Winchester, Rugby, Westminster, Marlborough, The Charterhouse. Crown 8vo, 6s.

OWEN, F. M.—John Keats : a Study. Crown 8vo, 6s.

OWEN, Rev. Robert, B.D.—Sanctorale Catholicum ; or, Book of Saints. With Notes, Critical, Exegetical, and Historical. Demy 8vo, 18s.

c

OXENHAM, Rev. F. Nutcombe.—**What is the Truth as to Ever--lasting Punishment.** Part II. Being an Historical Inquiry into the Witness and Weight of certain Anti-Origenist Councils. Crown 8vo, 2*s.* 6*d.*

OXONIENSES.—**Romanism, Protestantism, Anglicanism.** Being a Layman's View of some questions of the Day. Together with Remarks on Dr. Littledale's " Plain Reasons against joining the Church of Rome." Crown 8vo, 3*s.* 6*d.*

PALMER, the late William.—**Notes of a Visit to Russia in 1840-1841.** Selected and arranged by JOHN H. CARDINAL NEWMAN, with portrait. Crown 8vo, 8*s.* 6*d.*

Parchment Library. Choicely Printed on hand-made paper, limp parchment antique, 6*s.* ; vellum, 7*s.* 6*d.* each volume.

English Lyrics.

The Sonnets of John Milton. Edited by MARK PATTISON. With Portrait after Vertue.

Poems by Alfred Tennyson. 2 vols. With minature frontis-pieces by W. B. Richmond.

French Lyrics. Selected and Annotated by GEORGE SAINTS-BURY. With a minature frontispiece designed and etched by H. G. Glindoni.

The Fables of Mr. John Gay. With Memoir by AUSTIN DOBSON, and an etched portrait from an unfinished Oil Sketch by Sir Godfrey Kneller.

Select Letters of Percy Bysshe Shelley. Edited, with an Introduction, by RICHARD GARNETT.

The Christian Year. Thoughts in Verse for the Sundays and Holy Days throughout the Year. With Miniature Portrait of the Rev. J. Keble, after a Drawing by G. Richmond, R.A.

Shakspere's Works. Complete in Twelve Volumes.

Eighteenth Century Essays. Selected and Edited by AUSTIN DOBSON. With a Miniature Frontispiece by R. Caldecott.

Q. Horati Flacci Opera. Edited by F. A. CORNISH, Assistant Master at Eton. With a Frontispiece after a design by L. Alma Tadema, etched by Leopold Lowenstam.

Edgar Allan Poe's Poems. With an Essay on his Poetry by ANDREW LANG, and a Frontispiece by Linley Sambourne.

Shakspere's Sonnets. Edited by EDWARD DOWDEN. With a Frontispiece etched by Leopold Lowenstam, after the Death Mask.

English Odes. Selected by EDMUND W. GOSSE. With Frontis-piece on India paper by Hamo Thornycroft, A.R.A.

Of the Imitation of Christ. By THOMAS À KEMPIS. A revised Translation. With Frontispiece on India paper, from a Design by W. B. Richmond.

Parchment Library—*continued*.

> Tennyson's The Princess: a Medley. With a Miniature Frontispiece by H. M. Paget, and a Tailpiece in Outline by Gordon Browne.

> Poems: Selected from PERCY BYSSHE SHELLEY. Dedicated to Lady Shelley. With a Preface by RICHARD GARNETT and a Miniature Frontispiece.

> Tennyson's "In Memoriam." With a Miniature Portrait in *eau-forte* by Le Rat, after a Photograph by the late Mrs. Cameron.

PARSLOE, *Joseph*.—Our Railways. Sketches, Historical and Descriptive. With Practical Information as to Fares and Rates, etc., and a Chapter on Railway Reform. Crown 8vo, 6s.

PAUL, C. *Kegan*.—Biographical Sketches. Printed on hand-made paper, bound in buckram. Second Edition. Crown 8vo, 7s. 6d.

PAUL, *Alexander*.—Short Parliaments. A History of the National Demand for frequent General Elections. Small crown 8vo, 3s. 6d.

PEARSON, *Rev. S.*—Week-day Living. A Book for Young Men and Women. Second Edition. Crown 8vo, 5s.

PENRICE, *Maj. J., B.A.*—A Dictionary and Glossary of the Ko-ran. With Copious Grammatical References and Explanations of the Text. 4to, 21s.

PESCHEL, *Dr. Oscar*.—The Races of Man and their Geographical Distribution. Large crown 8vo, 9s.

PETERS, *F. H.*—The Nicomachean Ethics of Aristotle. Translated by. Crown 8vo, 6s.

PHIPSON, *E.*—The Animal Lore of Shakspeare's Time. Including Quadrupeds, Birds, Reptiles, Fish and Insects. Large post 8vo, 9s.

PIDGEON, *D.*—An Engineer's Holiday; or, Notes of a Round Trip from Long. 0° to 0°. New and Cheaper Edition. Large crown 8vo, 7s. 6d.

PRICE, *Prof. Bonamy*.—Currency and Banking. Crown 8vo, 6s.

> Chapters on Practical Political Economy. Being the Substance of Lectures delivered before the University of Oxford. New and Cheaper Edition. Large post 8vo, 5s.

Pulpit Commentary, The. (Old Testament Series.) Edited by the Rev. J. S. EXELL and the Rev. Canon H. D. M. SPENCE.

> Genesis. By the Rev. T. WHITELAW, M.A.; with Homilies by the Very Rev. J. F. MONTGOMERY, D.D., Rev. Prof. R. A. REDFORD, M.A., LL.B., Rev. F. HASTINGS, Rev. W. RODERTS, M.A. An Introduction to the Study of the Old Testament by the Venerable Archdeacon FARRAR, D.D., F.R.S.; and Introductions to the Pentateuch by the Right Rev. H. COTTERILL, D.D., and Rev. T. WHITELAW, M.A. Seventh Edition. 1 vol., 15s.

Pulpit Commentary, The—*continued.*

Exodus. By the Rev. Canon RAWLINSON. With Homilies by Rev. J. ORR, Rev. D. YOUNG, Rev. C. A. GOODHART, Rev. J. URQUHART, and the Rev. H. T. ROBJOHNS. Third Edition. 2 vols., 18*s.*

Leviticus. By the Rev. Prebendary MEYRICK, M.A. With Introductions by the Rev. R. COLLINS, Rev. Professor A. CAVE, and Homilies by Rev. Prof. REDFORD, LL.B., Rev. J. A. MACDONALD, Rev. W. CLARKSON, Rev. S. R. ALDRIDGE, LL.B., and Rev. McCHEYNE EDGAR. Fourth Edition. 15*s.*

Numbers. By the Rev. R. WINTERBOTHAM, LL.B.; with Homilies by the Rev. Professor W. BINNIE, D.D., Rev. E. S. PROUT, M.A., Rev. D. YOUNG, Rev. J. WAITE, and an Introduction by the Rev. THOMAS WHITELAW, M.A. Fourth Edition. 15*s.*

Deuteronomy. By the Rev. W. L. ALEXANDER, D.D. With Homilies by Rev. C. CLEMANCE, D.D., Rev. J. ORR, B.D., Rev. R. M. EDGAR, M.A., Rev. D. DAVIES, M.A. Third edition. 15*s.*

Joshua. By Rev. J. J. LIAS, M.A.; with Homilies by Rev. S. R. ALDRIDGE, LL.B., Rev. R. GLOVER, Rev. E. DE PRESSENSÉ, D.D., Rev. J. WAITE, B.A., Rev. F. W. ADENEY, M.A.; and an Introduction by the Rev. A. PLUMMER, M.A. Fifth Edition. 12*s. 6d.*

Judges and Ruth. By the Bishop of Bath and Wells, and Rev. J. MORRISON, D.D.; with Homilies by Rev. A. F. MUIR, M.A., Rev. W. F. ADENEY, M.A., Rev. W. M. STATHAM, and Rev. Professor J. THOMSON, M.A. Fourth Edition. 10*s. 6d.*

1 Samuel. By the Very Rev. R. P. SMITH, D.D.; with Homilies by Rev. DONALD FRASER, D.D., Rev. Prof. CHAPMAN, and Rev. B. DALE. Sixth Edition. 15*s.*

1 Kings. By the Rev. JOSEPH HAMMOND, LL.B. With Homilies by the Rev. E. DE PRESSENSÉ, D.D., Rev. J. WAITE, B.A., Rev. A. ROWLAND, LL.B., Rev. J. A. MACDONALD, and Rev. J. URQUHART. Fourth Edition. 15*s.*

Ezra, Nehemiah, and Esther. By Rev. Canon G. RAWLINSON, M.A.; with Homilies by Rev. Prof. J. R. THOMSON, M.A., Rev. Prof. R. A. REDFORD, LL.B., M.A., Rev. W. S. LEWIS, M.A., Rev. J. A. MACDONALD, Rev. A. MACKENNAL, B.A., Rev. W. CLARKSON, B.A., Rev. F. HASTINGS, Rev. W. DINWIDDIE, LL.B., Rev. Prof. ROWLANDS, B.A., Rev. G. WOOD, B.A., Rev. Prof. P. C. BARKER, LL.B., M.A., and the Rev. J. S. EXELL. Sixth Edition. 1 vol., 12*s. 6d.*

Jeremiah. By the Rev. J. K. CHEYNE, M.A.; with Homilies by the Rev. W. F. ADENEY, M.A., Rev. A. F. MUIR, M.A., Rev. S. CONWAY, B.A., Rev. J. WAITE, B.A., and Rev. D. YOUNG, B.A. Vol. I., 15*s.*

Pulpit Commentary, The. (New Testament Series.)
St. Mark. By Very Rev. E. BICKERSTETH, D.D., Dean of Lichfield ; with Homilies by Rev. Prof. THOMSON, M.A., Rev. Prof. GIVEN, M.A., Rev. Prof. JOHNSON, M.A., Rev. A. ROWLAND, B.A., LL.B., Rev. A. MUIR, and Rev. R. GREEN. 2 vols. Third Edition. 21*s.*

PUSEY, Dr.—Sermons for the Church's Seasons from Advent to Trinity. Selected from the Published Sermons of the late EDWARD BOUVERIE PUSEY, D.D. Crown 8vo, 5*s.*

QUILTER, Harry.—" The Academy," 1872-1882.

RADCLIFFE, Frank R. Y.—The New Politicus. Small crown 8vo, 2*s. 6d.*

Realities of the Future Life. Small crown 8vo, 1*s. 6d.*

RENDELL, J. M.—Concise Handbook of the Island of Madeira. With Plan of Funchal and Map of the Island. Fcap. 8vo, 1*s. 6d.*

REYNOLDS, Rev. J. W.—The Supernatural in Nature. A Verification by Free Use of Science. Third Edition, Revised and Enlarged. Demy 8vo, 14*s.*

The Mystery of Miracles. Third and Enlarged Edition. Crown 8vo, 6*s.*

RIBOT, Prof. Th.—Heredity : A Psychological Study on its Phenomena, its Laws, its Causes, and its Consequences. Large crown 8vo, 9*s.*

ROBERTSON, The late Rev. F. W., M.A.—Life and Letters of. Edited by the Rev. STOPFORD BROOKE, M.A.
I. Two vols., uniform with the Sermons. With Steel Portrait. Crown 8vo, 7*s. 6d.*
II. Library Edition, in Demy 8vo, with Portrait. 12*s.*
III. A Popular Edition, in 1 vol. Crown 8vo, 6*s.*

Sermons. Four Series. Small crown 8vo, 3*s. 6d.* each.

The Human Race, and other Sermons. Preached at Cheltenham, Oxford, and Brighton. New and Cheaper Edition. Crown 8vo, 3*s. 6d.*

Notes on Genesis. New and Cheaper Edition. Crown 8vo, 3*s. 6d.*

Expository Lectures on St. Paul's Epistles to the Corinthians. A New Edition. Small crown 8vo, 5*s.*

Lectures and Addresses, with other Literary Remains. A New Edition. Crown 8vo, 5*s.*

An Analysis of Mr. Tennyson's "In Memoriam." (Dedicated by Permission to the Poet-Laureate.) Fcap. 8vo, 2*s.*

The Education of the Human Race. Translated from the German of GOTTHOLD EPHRAIM LESSING. Fcap. 8vo, 2*s. 6d.*

The above Works can also be had, bound in half morocco.

*** A Portrait of the late Rev. F. W. Robertson, mounted for framing, can be had, 2*s. 6d.*

Rosmini Serbati (Life of). By G. STUART MACWALTER. 2 vols.
8vo. [Vol. I. now ready, 12*s*.

Rosmini's Origin of Ideas. Translated from the Fifth Italian
Edition of the Nuovo Saggio *Sull' origine delle idee*. 3 vols.
Demy 8vo, cloth. [Vols. I. and II. now ready, 16*s*. each.

Rosmini's Philosophical System. Translated, with a Sketch of
the Author's Life, Bibliography, Introduction, and Notes by
THOMAS DAVIDSON. Demy 8vo, 16*s*.

RULE, Martin, M.A.—**The Life and Times of St. Anselm,
Archbishop of Canterbury and Primate of the
Britains.** 2 vols. Demy 8vo, 21*s*.

SALVATOR, Archduke Ludwig.—**Levkosia, the Capital of Cyprus.**
Crown 4to, 10*s*. 6*d*.

SAMUEL, Sydney M.—**Jewish Life in the East.** Small crown
8vo, 3*s*. 6*d*.

SAYCE, Rev. Archibald Henry.—**Introduction to the Science of
Language.** 2 vols. Second Edition. Large post 8vo, 25*s*.

Scientific Layman. The New Truth and the Old Faith : are they
Incompatible ? Demy 8vo, 10*s*. 6*d*.

SCOONES, W. Baptiste.—**Four Centuries of English Letters :**
A Selection of 350 Letters by 150 Writers, from the Period of the
Paston Letters to the Present Time. Third Edition. **Large**
crown 8vo, 6*s*.

SHILLITO, Rev. Joseph.—**Womanhood :** its Duties, Temptations,
and Privileges. A Book for Young Women. Third Edition.
Crown 8vo, 3*s*. 6*d*.

SHIPLEY, Rev. Orby, M.A.—**Principles of the Faith in Rela-
tion to Sin.** Topics for Thought in Times of Retreat.
Eleven Addresses delivered during a Retreat of Three Days to
Persons living in the World. Demy 8vo, 12*s*.

Sister Augustine, Superior of the Sisters of Charity at the St.
Johannis Hospital at Bonn. Authorised Translation by HANS
THARAU, from the German "Memorials of AMALIE VON
LASAULX." Cheap Edition. Large crown 8vo, 4*s*. 6*d*.

SMITH, Edward, M.D., LL.B., F.R.S.—**Tubercular Consump-
tion in its Early and Remediable Stages.** Second
Edition. Crown 8vo, 6*s*.

SPEDDING, James.—**Reviews and Discussions, Literary,
Political, and Historical not relating to Bacon.** Demy
8vo, 12*s*. 6*d*.

Evenings with a Reviewer ; or, Bacon and Macaulay.
With a Prefatory Notice by G. S. VENABLES, Q.C. 2 vols.
Demy 8vo, 18*s*.

STAPFER, Paul.—Shakspeare and Classical Antiquity : Greek and Latin Antiquity as presented in Shakspeare's Plays. Translated by EMILY J. CAREY. Large post 8vo, 12*s.*

STEVENSON, Rev. W. F.—Hymns for the Church and Home. Selected and Edited by the Rev. W. FLEMING STEVENSON.
> The Hymn Book consists of Three Parts :—I. For Public Worship.—II. For Family and Private Worship.—III. For Children.

** Published in various forms and prices, the latter ranging from 8*d.* to 6*s.*
> Lists and full particulars will be furnished on application to the Publishers.

STEVENSON, Robert Louis.—Travels with a Donkey in the Cevennes. With Frontispiece by Walter Crane. Small crown 8vo, 2*s.* 6*d.*

> An Inland Voyage. With Frontispiece by Walter Crane. Small Crown 8vo, 2*s.* 6*d.*

> Virginibus Puerisque, and other Papers. Crown 8vo, 6*s.*

Stray Papers on Education, and Scenes from School Life. By B. H. Small crown 8vo, 3*s.* 6*d.*

STRECKER-WISLICENUS.—Organic Chemistry. Translated and Edited, with Extensive Additions, by W. R. HODGKINSON, Ph.D., and A. J. GREENAWAY, F.I.C. Demy 8vo, 21*s.*

SULLY, James, M.A.—Pessimism : a History and a Criticism. Second Edition. Demy 8vo, 14*s.*

SWEDENBORG, Eman.—De Cultu et Amore Dei ubi Agitur de Telluris ortu, Paradiso et Vivario, tum de Primogeniti Seu Adami Nativitate Infantia, et Amore. Crown 8vo, 5*s.*

SYME, David.—Representative Government in England. Its Faults and Failures. Second Edition. Large crown 8vo, 6*s.*

TAYLOR, Rev. Isaac.—The Alphabet. An Account of the Origin and Development of Letters. With numerous Tables and Facsimiles. 2 vols. Demy 8vo, 36*s.*

Thirty Thousand Thoughts. Edited by the Rev. CANON SPENCE, Rev. J. S. EXELL, Rev. CHARLES NEIL, and Rev. JACOB STEPHENSON. 6 vols. Super royal 8vo.
> [Vol. I. now ready, 16*s.*

THOM, J. Hamilton.—Laws of Life after the Mind of Christ. Second Edition. Crown 8vo, 7*s.* 6*d.*

THOMSON, J. Turnbull.—Social Problems; or, An Inquiry into the Laws of Influence. With Diagrams. Demy 8vo, 10*s.* 6*d.*

TIDMAN, Paul F.—Gold and Silver Money. Part I.—A Plain Statement. Part II.—Objections Answered. Third Edition. Crown 8vo, 1*s.*

TIPPLE, Rev. S. A.—Sunday Mornings at Norwood. Prayers and Sermons. Crown 8vo, 6*s.*

TODHUNTER, Dr. J.—A Study of Shelley. Crown 8vo, 7*s.*

TREMENHEERE, Hugh Seymour, C.B.— A Manual of the Principles of Government, as set forth by the Authorities of Ancient and Modern Times. New and Enlarged Edition. Crown 8vo, 5*s.*

TUKE, Daniel Hack, M.D., F.R.C.P.—Chapters in the History of the Insane in the British Isles. With 4 Illustrations. Large crown 8vo, 12*s.*

TWINING, Louisa.—Workhouse Visiting and Management during Twenty-Five Years. Small crown 8vo, 3*s.* 6*d.*

TYLER, J.—The Mystery of Being: or, What Do We Know ? Small crown 8vo, 3*s.* 6*d.*

UPTON, Major R. D.—Gleanings from the Desert of Arabia. Large post 8vo, 10*s.* 6*d.*

VACUUS, Viator.—Flying South. Recollections of France and its Littoral. Small crown 8vo, 3*s.* 6*d.*

VAUGHAN, H. Halford.—New Readings and Renderings of Shakespeare's Tragedies. 2 vols. Demy 8vo, 25*s.*

VILLARI, Professor.—Niccolò Machiavelli and his Times. Translated by Linda Villari. 4 vols. Large post 8vo, 48*s.*

VILLIERS, The Right Hon. C. P.—Free Trade Speeches of. With Political Memoir. Edited by a Member of the Cobden Club. 2 vols. With Portrait. Demy 8vo, 25*s.*

VOGT, Lieut.-Col. Hermann.—The Egyptian War of 1882. A translation. With Map and Plans. Large crown 8vo, 6*s.*

VOLCKXSOM, E. W. V.—Catechism of Elementary Modern Chemistry. Small crown 8vo, 3*s.*

VYNER, Lady Mary.—Every Day a Portion. Adapted from the Bible and the Prayer Book, for the Private Devotion of those living in Widowhood. Collected and Edited by Lady Mary Vyner. Square crown 8vo, 5*s.*

WALDSTEIN, Charles, Ph.D.—The Balance of Emotion and Intellect ; an Introductory Essay to the Study of Philosophy. Crown 8vo, 6*s.*

WALLER, Rev. C. B.—The Apocalypse, reviewed under the Light of the Doctrine of the Unfolding Ages, and the Restitution of All Things. Demy 8vo, 12*s.*

WALPOLE, Chas. George.—History of Ireland from the Earliest Times to the Union with Great Britain. With 5 Maps and Appendices. Crown 8vo, 10s. 6d.

WALSHE, Walter Hayle, M.D.—Dramatic Singing Physiologically Estimated. Crown 8vo, 3s. 6d.

WEDMORE, Frederick.—The Masters of Genre Painting. With Sixteen Illustrations. Crown 8vo, 7s. 6d.

WHEWELL, William, D.D.—His Life and Selections from his Correspondence. By Mrs. STAIR DOUGLAS. With a Portrait from a Painting by Samuel Laurence. Demy 8vo, 21s.

WHITNEY, Prof. William Dwight.—Essentials of English Grammar, for the Use of Schools. Crown 8vo, 3s. 6d.

WILLIAMS, Rowland, D.D.—Psalms, Litanies, Counsels, and Collects for Devout Persons. Edited by his Widow. New and Popular Edition. Crown 8vo, 3s. 6d.

Stray Thoughts Collected from the Writings of the late Rowland Williams, D.D. Edited by his Widow. Crown 8vo, 3s. 6d.

WILLIS, R., M.A.—William Harvey. A History of the Discovery of the Circulation of the Blood : with a Portrait of Harvey after Faithorne. Demy 8vo, 14s.

WILSON, Sir Erasmus.—Egypt of the Past. With Chromo-lithograph and numerous Illustrations in the text. Second Edition, Revised. Crown 8vo, 12s.

The Recent Archaic Discovery of Egyptian Mummies at Thebes. A Lecture. Crown 8vo, 1s. 6d.

WILSON, Lieut.-Col. C. T.—The Duke of Berwick, Marshall of France, 1702-1734. Demy 8vo, 15s.

WOLTMANN, Dr. Alfred, and WOERMANN, Dr. Karl.—History of Painting. Edited by SIDNEY COLVIN. Vol. I. Painting in Antiquity and the Middle Ages. With numerous Illustrations. Medium 8vo, 28s. ; bevelled boards, gilt leaves, 30s.

Word was Made Flesh. Short Family Readings on the Epistles for each Sunday of the Christian Year. Demy 8vo, 10s. 6d.

WREN, Sir Christopher.—His Family and His Times. With Original Letters, and a Discourse on Architecture hitherto unpublished. By LUCY PHILLIMORE. With Portrait. Demy 8vo, 14s.

YOUMANS, Eliza A.—First Book of Botany. Designed to Cultivate the Observing Powers of Children. With 300 Engravings. New and Cheaper Edition. Crown 8vo, 2s. 6d.

YOUMANS, Edward L., M.D.—A Class Book of Chemistry, on the Basis of the New System. With 200 Illustrations. Crown 8vo, 5s.

THE INTERNATIONAL SCIENTIFIC SERIES.

I. **Forms of Water:** a Familiar Exposition of the Origin and Phenomena of Glaciers. By J. Tyndall, LL.D., F.R.S. With 25 Illustrations. Eighth Edition. Crown 8vo, 5s.

II. **Physics and Politics**; or, Thoughts on the Application of the Principles of "Natural Selection" and "Inheritance" to Political Society. By Walter Bagehot. Sixth Edition. Crown 8vo, 4s.

III. **Foods.** By Edward Smith, M.D., LL.B., F.R.S. With numerous Illustrations. Eighth Edition. Crown 8vo, 5s.

IV. **Mind and Body:** the Theories of their Relation. By Alexander Bain, LL.D. With Four Illustrations. Seventh Edition. Crown 8vo, 4s.

V. **The Study of Sociology.** By Herbert Spencer. Eleventh Edition. Crown 8vo, 5s.

VI. **On the Conservation of Energy.** By Balfour Stewart, M.A., LL.D., F.R.S. With 14 Illustrations. Sixth Edition. Crown 8vo, 5s.

VII. **Animal Locomotion**; or Walking, Swimming, and Flying. By J. B. Pettigrew, M.D., F.R.S., etc. With 130 Illustrations. Third Edition. Crown 8vo, 5s.

VIII. **Responsibility in Mental Disease.** By Henry Maudsley, M.D. Fourth Edition. Crown 8vo, 5s.

IX. **The New Chemistry.** By Professor J. P. Cooke. With 31 Illustrations. Seventh Edition. Crown 8vo, 5s.

X. **The Science of Law.** By Professor Sheldon Amos. Fifth Edition. Crown 8vo, 5s.

XI. **Animal Mechanism:** a Treatise on Terrestrial and Aerial Locomotion. By Professor E. J. Marey. With 117 Illustrations. Third Edition. Crown 8vo, 5s.

XII. **The Doctrine of Descent and Darwinism.** By Professor Oscar Schmidt. With 26 Illustrations. Fifth Edition. Crown 8vo, 5s.

XIII. **The History of the Conflict between Religion and Science.** By J. W. Draper, M.D., LL.D. Seventeenth Edition. Crown 8vo, 5s.

XIV. **Fungi:** their Nature, Influences, Uses, etc. By M. C. Cooke, M.D., LL.D. Edited by the Rev. M. J. Berkeley, M.A., F.L.S. With numerous Illustrations. Third Edition. Crown 8vo, 5s.

XV. **The Chemical Effects of Light and Photography.** By Dr. Hermann Vogel. Translation thoroughly Revised. With 100 Illustrations. Fourth Edition. Crown 8vo, 5s.

XVI. **The Life and Growth of Language.** By Professor William Dwight Whitney. Fourth Edition. Crown 8vo, 5*s.*

XVII. **Money and the Mechanism of Exchange.** By W. Stanley Jevons, M.A., F.R.S. Sixth Edition. Crown 8vo, 5*s.*

XVIII. **The Nature of Light.** With a General Account of Physical Optics. By Dr. Eugene Lommel. With 188 Illustrations and a Table of Spectra in Chromo-lithography. Third Edition. Crown 8vo, 5*s.*

XIX. **Animal Parasites and Messmates.** By Monsieur Van Beneden. With 83 Illustrations. Third Edition. Crown 8vo, 5*s.*

XX. **Fermentation.** By Professor Schützenberger. With 28 Illustrations. Third Edition. Crown 8vo, 5*s.*

XXI. **The Five Senses of Man.** By Professor Bernstein. With 91 Illustrations. Fourth Edition. Crown 8vo, 5*s.*

XXII. **The Theory of Sound in its Relation to Music.** By Professor Pietro Blaserna. With numerous Illustrations. Third Edition. Crown 8vo, 5*s.*

XXIII. **Studies in Spectrum Analysis.** By J. Norman Lockyer, F.R.S. With six photographic Illustrations of Spectra, and numerous engravings on Wood. Third Edition. Crown 8vo, 6*s.* 6*d.*

XXIV. **A History of the Growth of the Steam Engine.** By Professor R. H. Thurston. With numerous Illustrations. Third Edition. Crown 8vo, 6*s.* 6*d.*

XXV. **Education as a Science.** By Alexander Bain, LL.D. Fourth Edition. Crown 8vo, 5*s.*

XXVI. **The Human Species.** By Professor A. de Quatrefages. Third Edition. Crown 8vo, 5*s.*

XXVII. **Modern Chromatics.** With Applications to Art and Industry. By Ogden N. Rood. With 130 original Illustrations. Second Edition. Crown 8vo, 5*s.*

XXVIII. **The Crayfish :** an Introduction to the Study of Zoology. By Professor T. H. Huxley. With 82 Illustrations. Third Edition. Crown 8vo, 5*s.*

XXIX. **The Brain as an Organ of Mind.** By H. Charlton Bastian, M.D. With numerous Illustrations. Third Edition. Crown 8vo, 5*s.*

XXX. **The Atomic Theory.** By Prof. Wurtz. Translated by G. Cleminshaw, F.C.S. Third Edition. Crown 8vo, 5*s.*

XXXI. **The Natural Conditions of Existence as they affect Animal Life.** By Karl Semper. With 2 Maps and 106 Woodcuts. Third Edition. Crown 8vo, 5*s.*

XXXII. **General Physiology of Muscles and Nerves.** By Prof. J. Rosenthal. Third Edition. With Illustrations. Crown 8vo, 5s.

XXXIII. **Sight:** an Exposition of the Principles of Monocular and Binocular Vision. By Joseph le Conte, LL.D. Second Edition. With 132 Illustrations. Crown 8vo, 5s.

XXXIV. **Illusions:** a Psychological Study. By James Sully. Second Edition. Crown 8vo, 5s.

XXXV. **Volcanoes: what they are and what they teach.** By Professor J. W. Judd, F.R.S. With 92 Illustrations on Wood. Second Edition. Crown 8vo, 5s.

XXXVI. **Suicide:** an Essay in Comparative Moral Statistics. By Prof. E. Morselli. Second Edition. With Diagrams. Crown 8vo, 5s.

XXXVII. **The Brain and its Functions.** By J. Luys. With Illustrations. Second Edition. Crown 8vo, 5s.

XXXVIII. **Myth and Science:** an Essay. By Tito Vignoli. Crown 8vo, 5s.

XXXIX. **The Sun.** By Professor Young. With Illustrations. Second Edition. Crown 8vo, 5s.

XL. **Ants, Bees, and Wasps:** a Record of Observations on the Habits of the Social Hymenoptera. By Sir John Lubbock, Bart., M.P. With 5 Chromo-lithographic Illustrations. Sixth Edition. Crown 8vo, 5s.

XLI. **Animal Intelligence.** By G. J. Romanes, LL.D., F.R.S. Third Edition. Crown 8vo, 5s.

XLII. **The Concepts and Theories of Modern Physics.** By J. B. Stallo. Second Edition. Crown 8vo, 5s.

XLIII. **Diseases of the Memory;** An Essay in the Positive Psychology. By Prof. Th. Ribot. Second Edition. Crown 8vo, 5s.

XLIV. **Man before Metals.** By N. Joly, with 148 Illustrations. Third Edition. Crown 8vo, 5s.

XLV. **The Science of Politics.** By Prof. Sheldon Amos. Second Edition. Crown 8vo, 5s.

XLVI. **Elementary Meteorology.** By Robert H. Scott. Second Edition. With Numerous Illustrations. Crown 8vo, 5s.

XLVII. **The Organs of Speech and their Application in the Formation of Articulate Sounds.** By George Hermann Von Meyer. With 47 Woodcuts. Crown 8vo, 5s.

XLVIII. **Fallacies.** A View of Logic from the Practical Side. By Alfred Sidgwick.

MILITARY WORKS.

BARRINGTON, Capt. J. T.—England on the Defensive ; or, the Problem of Invasion Critically Examined. Large crown 8vo, with Map, 7s. 6d.

BRACKENBURY, Col. C. B., R.A., C.B.—Military Handbooks for Regimental Officers.

    I. Military Sketching and Reconnaissance. By Col. F. J. Hutchison, and Major H. G. MacGregor. Fourth Edition. With 15 Plates. Small 8vo, 6s.

    II. The Elements of Modern Tactics Practically applied to English Formations. By Lieut.-Col. Wilkinson Shaw. Fourth Edition. With 25 Plates and Maps. Small crown 8vo, 9s.

    III. Field Artillery. Its Equipment, Organization and Tactics. By Major Sisson C. Pratt, R.A. With 12 Plates. Second Edition. Small crown 8vo, 6s.

    IV. The Elements of Military Administration. First Part : Permanent System of Administration. By Major J. W. Buxton. Small crown 8vo. 7s. 6d.

    V. Military Law : Its Procedure and Practice. By Major Sisson C. Pratt, R.A. Small crown 8vo.

BROOKE, Major, C. K.—A System of Field Training. Small crown 8vo, cloth limp, 2s.

CLERY, C., Lieut.-Col.—Minor Tactics. With 26 Maps and Plans. Sixth and Cheaper Edition, Revised. Crown 8vo, 9s.

COLVILE, Lieut.-Col. C. F.—Military Tribunals. Sewed, 2s. 6d.

HARRISON, Lieut.-Col. R.—The Officer's Memorandum Book for Peace and War. Third Edition. Oblong 32mo, roan, with pencil, 3s. 6d.

Notes on Cavalry Tactics, Organisation, etc. By a Cavalry Officer. With Diagrams. Demy 8vo, 12s.

PARR, Capt. H. Hallam, C.M.G.—The Dress, Horses, and Equipment of Infantry and Staff Officers. Crown 8vo, 1s.

SCHAW, Col. H.—The Defence and Attack of Positions and Localities. Second Edition, Revised and Corrected. Crown 8vo, 3s. 6d.

SHADWELL, Maj.-Gen., C.B.—Mountain Warfare. Illustrated by the Campaign of 1799 in Switzerland. Being a Translation of the Swiss Narrative compiled from the Works of the Archduke Charles, Jomini, and others. Also of Notes by General H. Dufour on the Campaign of the Valtelline in 1635. With Appendix, Maps, and Introductory Remarks. Demy 8vo, 16s.

STUBBS, Lieut.-Col. F. W.—**The Regiment of Bengal Artillery.** The History of its Organisation, Equipment, and War Services. Compiled from Published Works, Official Records, and various Private Sources. With numerous Maps and Illustrations. 2 vols. Demy 8vo, 32*s*.

POETRY.

ADAM OF ST. VICTOR.—**The Liturgical Poetry of Adam of St. Victor.** From the text of GAUTIER. With Translations into English in the Original Metres, and Short Explanatory Notes, by DIGBY S. WRANGHAM, M.A. 3 vols. Crown 8vo, printed on hand-made paper, boards, 21*s*.

AUCHMUTY, A. C.—**Poems of English Heroism :** From Brunanburh to Lucknow ; from Athelstan to Albert. Small crown 8vo, 1*s*. 6*d*.

AVIA.—**The Odyssey of Homer.** Done into English Verse by. Fcap. 4to, 15*s*.

BANKS, Mrs. G. L.—**Ripples and Breakers :** Poems. Square 8vo, 5*s*.

BARNES, William.—**Poems of Rural Life, in the Dorset Dialect.** New Edition, complete in one vol. Crown 8vo, 8*s*. 6*d*.

BAYNES, Rev. Canon H. R.—**Home Songs for Quiet Hours.** Fourth and Cheaper Edition. Fcap. 8vo, cloth, 2*s*. 6*d*.
   *** This may also be had handsomely bound in morocco with gilt edges.

BENNETT, C. Fletcher.—**Life Thoughts.** A New Volume of Poems. With Frontispiece. Small crown 8vo.

BEVINGTON, L. S.—**Key Notes.** Small crown 8vo, 5*s*.

BILLSON, C. J.—**The Acharnians of Aristophanes.** Crown 8vo, 3*s*. 6*d*.

BOWEN, H. C., M.A.—**Simple English Poems.** English Literature for Junior Classes. In Four Parts. Parts I., II., and III., 6*d*. each, and Part IV., 1*s*.

BRYANT, W. C.—**Poems.** Red-line Edition. With 24 Illustrations and Portrait of the Author. Crown 8vo, extra, 7*s*. 6*d*.
   A Cheap Edition, with Frontispiece. Small crown 8vo, 3*s*. 6*d*.

BYRNNE, E. Fairfax.—**Millicent :** a Poem. Small crown 8vo, 6*s*.

Calderon's Dramas : the Wonder-Working Magician — Life is a Dream—the Purgatory of St. Patrick. Translated by DENIS FLORENCE MACCARTHY. Post 8vo, 10*s*.

Castilian Brothers (The), Chateaubriant, Waldemar: Three Tragedies; and **The Rose of Sicily:** a Drama. By the Author of "Ginevra," &c. Crown 8vo, 6s.

Chronicles of Christopher Columbus. A Poem in 12 Cantos. By M. D. C. Crown 8vo, 7s. 6d.

CLARKE, Mary Cowden.—**Honey from the Weed.** Verses. Crown 8vo, 7s.

COLOMB, Colonel.—**The Cardinal Archbishop:** a Spanish Legend. In 29 Cancions. Small crown 8vo, 5s.

CONWAY, Hugh.—**A Life's Idylls.** Small crown 8vo, 3s. 6d.

COPPÉE, Francois.—**L'Exilée.** Done into English Verse, with the sanction of the Author, by I. O. L. Crown 8vo, vellum, 5s.

COXHEAD, Ethel.—**Birds and Babies.** Imp. 16mo. With 33 Illustrations. Gilt, 2s. 6d.

David Rizzio, Bothwell, and the Witch Lady. Three Tragedies by the author of "Ginevra," etc. Crown 8vo, 6s.

DAVIE, G. S., M.D.—**The Garden of Fragrance.** Being a complete translation of the Bostán of Sádi from the original Persian into English Verse. Crown 8vo, 7s. 6d.

DAVIES, T. Hart.—**Catullus.** Translated into English Verse. Crown 8vo, 6s.

DE VERE, Aubrey.—**The Foray of Queen Meave,** and other Legends of Ireland's Heroic Age. Small crown 8vo, 5s.

Legends of the Saxon Saints. Small crown 8vo, 6s.

DILLON, Arthur.—**River Songs and other Poems.** With 13 autotype Illustrations from designs by Margery May. Fcap. 4to, cloth extra, gilt leaves, 10s. 6d.

DOBELL, Mrs. Horace.—**Ethelstone, Eveline,** and other Poems. Crown 8vo, 6s.

DOBSON, Austin.—**Old World Idylls** and other Poems. 18mo, cloth extra, gilt tops, 6s.

DOMET, Alfred.—**Ranolf and Amohia.** A Dream of Two Lives. New Edition, Revised. 2 vols. Crown 8vo, 12s.

Dorothy: a Country Story in Elegiac Verse. With Preface. Demy 8vo, 5s.

DOWDEN, Edward, LL.D.—**Shakspere's Sonnets.** With Introduction. Large post 8vo, 7s. 6d.

DOWNTON, Rev. H., M.A.—**Hymns and Verses.** Original and Translated. Small crown 8vo, 3s. 6d.

DUTT, Toru.—**A Sheaf Gleaned in French Fields.** New Edition. Demy 8vo, 10s. 6d.

EDMONDS, E. W.—**Hesperas.** Rhythm and Rhyme. Crown 8vo, 4*s.*

ELDRYTH, Maud.—**Margaret,** and other Poems. Small crown 8vo, 3*s. 6d.*

ELLIOTT, Ebenezer, The Corn Law Rhymer.—**Poems.** Edited by his son, the Rev. EDWIN ELLIOTT, of St. John's, Antigua. 2 vols. Crown 8vo, 18*s.*

English Odes. Selected, with a Critical Introduction by EDMUND W. GOSSE, and a miniature frontispiece by Hamo Thornycroft, A.R.A. Elzevir 8vo, limp parchment antique, 6*s.*; vellum, 7*s. 6d.*

EVANS, Anne.—**Poems and Music.** With Memorial Preface by ANN THACKERAY RITCHIE. Large crown 8vo, 7*s.*

GOSSE, Edmund W.—**New Poems.** Crown 8vo, 7*s. 6d.*

GRAHAM, William. **Two Fancies** and other Poems. Crown 8vo, 5*s.*

GRINDROD, Charles. **Plays from English History.** Crown 8vo, 7*s. 6d.*

GURNEY, Rev. Alfred.—**The Vision of the Eucharist,** and other Poems. Crown 8vo, 5*s.*

HELLON, H. G.—**Daphnis:** a Pastoral Poem. Small crown 8vo, 3*s. 6d.*

Herman Waldgrave: a Life's Drama. By the Author of "Ginevra," etc. Crown 8vo, 6*s.*

HICKEY, E. H.—**A Sculptor,** and other Poems. Small crown 8vo, 5*s.*

Horati Opera. Edited by F. A. CORNISH, Assistant Master at Eton. With a Frontispiece after a design by L. Alma Tadema, etched by Leopold Lowenstam. Parchment Library Edition, 6*s.*; vellum, 7*s. 6d.*

INGHAM, Sarson, C. J.—**Cædmon's Vision,** and other Poems. Small crown 8vo, 5*s.*

JENKINS, Rev. Canon.—**Alfonso Petrucci,** Cardinal and Conspirator: an Historical Tragedy in Five Acts. Small crown 8vo, 3*s. 6d.*

KING, Edward.—**Echoes from the Orient.** With Miscellaneous Poems. Small crown 8vo, 3*s. 6d.*

KING, Mrs. Hamilton.—**The Disciples.** Fifth Edition, with Portrait and Notes. Crown 8vo, 5*s.*

    A Book of Dreams. Crown 8vo, 5*s.*

LANG, A.—**XXXII Ballades in Blue China.** Elzevir 8vo, parchment, 5*s.*

LAWSON, Right Hon. Mr. Justice.—Hymni Usitati Latine Redditi: with other Verses. Small 8vo, parchment, 5*s.*

LEIGH, Arran and Isla.—Bellerophon. Small crown 8vo, 5*s.*

LEIGHTON, Robert.—Records, and other Poems. With Portrait. Small crown 8vo, 7*s.* 6*d.*

Lessings Nathan the Wise. Translated by EUSTACE K. CORBETT. Crown 8vo, 6*s.*

Living English Poets MDCCCLXXXII. With Frontispiece by Walter Crane. Second Edition. Large crown 8vo. Printed on hand-made paper. Parchment, 12*s.*, vellum, 15*s.*

LOCKER, F.—London Lyrics. A New and Cheaper Edition. Small crown 8vo, 2*s.* 6*d.*

Love in Idleness. A Volume of Poems. With an etching by W. B. Scott. Small crown 8vo, 5*s.*

Love Sonnets of Proteus. With Frontispiece by the Author. Elzevir 8vo, 5*s.*

LOWNDES, Henry.—Poems and Translations. Crown 8vo, 6*s.*

LUMSDEN, Lieut.-Col. H. W.—Beowulf: an Old English Poem. Translated into Modern Rhymes. Second Edition. Small crown 8vo, 5*s.*

Lyre and Star. Poems by the Author of "Ginevra," etc. Crown 8vo, 5*s.*

MACLEAN, Charles Donald.—Latin and Greek Verse Translations. Small crown 8vo, 2*s.*

MAGNUSSON, Eirikr, M.A., and PALMER, E. H., M.A.—Johan Ludvig Runeberg's Lyrical Songs, Idylls, and Epigrams. Fcap. 8vo, 5*s.*

M.D.C.—Chronicles of Christopher Columbus. A Poem in Twelve Cantos. Crown 8vo, 7*s.* 6*d.*

MEREDITH, Owen, The Earl of Lytton.—Lucile. New Edition. With 32 Illustrations. 16mo, 3*s.* 6*d.* Cloth extra, gilt edges, 4*s.* 6*d.*

MIDDLETON, The Lady.—Ballads. Square 16mo, 3*s.* 6*d.*

MORICE, Rev. F. D., M.A.—The Olympian and Pythian Odes of Pindar. A New Translation in English Verse. Crown 8vo, 7*s.* 6*d.*

MORRIS, Lewis.—Poetical Works of. New and Cheaper Editions, with Portrait. Complete in 3 vols., 5*s.* each.

Vol. I. contains "Songs of Two Worlds." Vol. II. contains "The Epic of Hades." Vol. III. contains "Gwen" and "The Ode of Life."

D

MORRIS, Lewis—continued.

The Epic of Hades. With 16 Autotype Illustrations, after the Drawings of the late George R. Chapman. 4to, cloth extra, gilt leaves, 25s.

The Epic of Hades. Presentation Edition. 4to, cloth extra, gilt leaves, 10s. 6d.

Ode of Life, The. Fourth Edition. Crown 8vo, 5s.

Songs Unsung. Fcap. 8vo.

MORSHEAD, E. D. A.—The House of Atreus. Being the Agamemnon, Libation-Bearers, and Furies of Æschylus. Translated into English Verse. Crown 8vo, 7s.

The Suppliant Maidens of Æschylus. Crown 8vo, 3s. 6d.

NADEN, Constance W.—Songs and Sonnets of Spring Time. Small crown 8vo, 5s.

NEWELL, E. J.—The Sorrows of Simona and Lyrical Verses. Small crown 8vo, 3s. 6d.

NOAKE, Major R. Compton.—The Bivouac ; or, Martial Lyrist. With an Appendix : Advice to the Soldier. Fcap. 8vo, 5s. 6d.

NOEL, The Hon. Roden.—A Little Child's Monument. Second Edition. Small crown 8vo, 3s. 6d.

NORRIS, Rev. Alfred.—The Inner and Outer Life. Poems. Fcap. 8vo, 6s.

O'HAGAN, John.—The Song of Roland. Translated into English Verse. New and Cheaper Edition. Crown 8vo, 5s.

PFEIFFER, Emily.—Glan Alarch : His Silence and Song : a Poem. Second Edition. Crown 8vo, 6s.

Gerard's Monument, and other Poems. Second Edition. Crown 8vo, 6s.

Quarterman's Grace, and other Poems. Crown 8vo, 5s.

Poems. Second Edition. Crown 8vo, 6s.

Sonnets and Songs. New Edition. 16mo, handsomely printed and bound in cloth, gilt edges, 4s.

Under the Aspens ; Lyrical and Dramatic. With Portrait. Crown 8vo, 6s.

PIKE, Warburton.—The Inferno of Dante Allighieri. Demy 8vo, 5s.

POE, Edgar Allan.—Poems. With an Essay on his Poetry by ANDREW LANG, and a Frontispiece by Linley Sambourne. Parchment Library Edition, 6s. ; vellum, 7s. 6d.

Rare Poems of the 16th and 17th Centuries. Edited W. J. LINTON. Crown 8vo, 5*s.*

RHOADES, James.—**The Georgics of Virgil.** Translated into English Verse. Small crown 8vo, 5*s.*

ROBINSON, A. Mary F.—**A Handful of Honeysuckle.** Fcap. 8vo, 3*s.* 6*d.*

    The Crowned Hippolytus. Translated from Euripides. With New Poems. Small crown 8vo, 5*s.*

SAUNDERS, John.—**Love's Martyrdom.** A Play and Poem. Small crown 8vo, 5*s.*

Schiller's Mary Stuart. German Text, with English Translation on opposite page by LEEDHAM WHITE. Crown 8vo, 6*s.*

SCOTT, George F. E.—**Theodora and other Poems.** Small 8vo, 3*s.* 6*d.*

SELKIRK, J. B.—**Poems.** Crown 8vo, 7*s.* 6*d.*

Shakspere's Sonnets. Edited by EDWARD DOWDEN. With a Frontispiece etched by Leopold Lowenstam, after the Death Mask. Parchment Library Edition, 6*s.* ; vellum, 7*s.* 6*d.*

Shakspere's Works. Complete in 12 Volumes. Parchment Library Edition, 6*s.* each ; vellum, 7*s.* 6*d.* each.

SHAW, W. F., M.A.—**Juvenal, Persius, Martial, and Catullus.** An Experiment in Translation. Crown 8vo, 5*s.*

SHELLEY, Percy Bysshe.—**Poems Selected from.** Dedicated to Lady Shelley. With Preface by RICHARD GARNETT. Parchment Library Edition, 6*s.* ; vellum, 7*s.* 6*d.*

Six Ballads about King Arthur. Crown 8vo, extra, gilt edges, 3*s.* 6*d.*

SLADEN, Douglas B.—**Frithjof and Ingebjorg, and** other Poems. Small crown 8vo, 5*s.*

TAYLOR, Sir H.—**Works.** Complete in Five Volumes. Crown 8vo, 30*s.*

    Philip Van Artevelde. Fcap. 8vo, 3*s.* 6*d.*

    The Virgin Widow, etc. Fcap. 8vo, 3*s.* 6*d.*

    The Statesman. Fcap. 8vo, 3*s.* 6*d.*

TENNYSON, Alfred.—Works Complete :—

    The Imperial Library Edition. Complete in 7 vols. Demy 8vo, 10*s.* 6*d.* each ; in Roxburgh binding, 12*s.* 6*d.* each.

    Author's Edition. In 7 vols. Post 8vo, gilt 43*s.* 6*d.* ; or half-morocco, Roxburgh style, 54*s.*

    Cabinet Edition. 13 vols. Each with Frontispiece. Fcap. 8vo, 2*s.* 6*d.* each.

    Cabinet Edition. 13 vols. Complete in handsome Ornamental Case. 35*s.*

TENNYSON, Alfred—continued.

The Royal Edition. In 1 vol. With 26 Illustrations and Portrait. Extra, bevelled boards, gilt leaves, 21*s.*

The Guinea Edition. Complete in 13 vols. neatly bound and enclosed in box, 21*s.* ; French morocco or parchment, 31*s. 6d.*

Shilling Edition. In 13 vols. pocket size, 1*s.* each, sewed.

The Crown Edition. Complete in 1 vol. strongly bound, 6*s.* ; extra gilt leaves, 7*s. 6d.* ; Roxburgh, half-morocco, 8*s. 6d.*
   ⁎⁎ Can also be had in a variety of other bindings.

In Memoriam. With a Miniature Portrait in *eau-forte* by Le Rat, after a Photograph by the late Mrs. Cameron. Parchment Library Edition, 6*s.* ; vellum, 7*s. 6d.*

The Princess. A Medley. With a Miniature Frontispiece by H. M. Paget, and a Tailpiece in Outline by Gordon Browne. Parchment Library Edition, 6*s.* ; vellum, 7*s. 6d.*

Original Editions :—

Poems. Small 8vo, 6*s.*

Maud, and other Poems. Small 8vo, 3*s. 6d.*

The Princess. Small 8vo, 3*s. 6d.*

Idylls of the King. Small 8vo, 5*s.*

Idylls of the King. Complete. Small 8vo, 6*s.*

The Holy Grail, and other Poems. Small 8vo, 4*s. 6d.*

Gareth and Lynette. Small 8vo, 3*s.*

Enoch Arden, etc. Small 8vo, 3*s. 6d.*

In Memoriam. Small 8vo, 4*s.*

Harold : a Drama. New Edition. Crown 8vo, 6*s.*

Queen Mary : a Drama. New Edition. Crown 8vo, 6*s.*

The Lover's Tale. Fcap. 8vo, 3*s. 6d.*

Ballads, and other Poems. Small 8vo, 5*s.*

Selections from the above Works. Super royal 16mo, 3*s. 6d.* ; gilt extra, 4*s.*

Songs from the above Works. 16mo, 2*s. 6d.*

Tennyson for the Young and for Recitation. Specially arranged. Fcap. 8vo, 1*s. 6d.*

The Tennyson Birthday Book. Edited by EMILY SHAKESPEAR. 32mo, limp, 2*s.* ; extra, 3*s.*
   ⁎⁎ A superior Edition; printed in red and black, on antique paper, specially prepared. Small crown 8vo, extra, gilt leaves, 5*s.* ; and in various calf and morocco bindings.

THORNTON, L. M.—The Son of Shelomith. Small crown 8vo, 3*s.* 6*d.*

TODHUNTER, Dr. J.—Laurella, and other Poems. Crown 8vo, 6*s.* 6*d.*

Forest Songs. Small crown 8vo, 3*s.* 6*d.*

The True Tragedy of Rienzi : a Drama. 3*s.* 6*d.*

Alcestis : a Dramatic Poem. Extra fcap. 8vo, 5*s.*

A Study of Shelley. Crown 8vo, 7*s.*

Translations from Dante, Petrarch, Michael Angelo, and Vittoria Colonna. Fcap. 8vo, 7*s.* 6*d.*

TURNER, Rev. C. Tennyson.—Sonnets, Lyrics, and Translations. Crown 8vo, 4*s.* 6*d.*

Collected Sonnets, Old and New. With Prefatory Poem by ALFRED TENNYSON ; also some Marginal Notes by S. T. COLERIDGE, and a Critical Essay by JAMES SPEDDING. Fcap. 8vo, 7*s.* 6*d.*

WALTERS, Sophia Lydia.—A Dreamer's Sketch Book. With 21 Illustrations by Percival Skelton, R. P. Leitch, W. H. J. Boot, and T. R. Pritchett. Engraved by J. D. Cooper. Fcap. 4to, 12*s.* 6*d.*

WEBSTER, Augusta.—In a Day : a Drama. Small crown 8vo, 2*s.* 6*d.*

Wet Days. By a Farmer. Small crown 8vo, 6*s.*

WILKINS, William.—Songs of Study. Crown 8vo, 6*s.*

WILLIAMS, J.—A Story of Three Years, and other Poems. Small crown 8vo, 3*s.* 6*d.*

YOUNGS, Ella Sharpe.—Paphus, and other Poems. Small crown 8vo, 3*s.* 6*d.*

WORKS OF FICTION IN ONE VOLUME.

BANKS, Mrs. G. L.—God's Providence House. New Edition. Crown 8vo, 3*s.* 6*d.*

HARDY, Thomas.—A Pair of Blue Eyes. Author of "Far from the Madding Crowd." New Edition. Crown 8vo, 6*s.*

The Return of the Native. New Edition. With Frontispiece. Crown 8vo, 6*s.*

INGELOW, Jean.—Off the Skelligs : a Novel. With Frontispiece. Second Edition. Crown 8vo, 6*s.*

MACDONALD, G.—Castle Warlock. A Novel. New and Cheaper Edition. Crown 8vo, 6*s.*

MACDONALD, G.—continued.

Malcolm. With Portrait of the Author engraved on Steel. Sixth Edition. Crown 8vo, 6s.

The Marquis of Lossie. Fourth Edition. With Frontispiece. Crown 8vo, 6s.

St. George and St. Michael. Third Edition. With Frontispiece. Crown 8vo, 6s.

PALGRAVE, W. Gifford.—**Hermann Agha**: an Eastern Narrative. Third Edition. Crown 8vo, 6s.

SHAW, Flora L.—**Castle Blair**; a Story of Youthful Lives. New and Cheaper Edition. Crown 8vo, 3s. 6d.

STRETTON, Hesba.—**Through a Needle's Eye**: a Story. New and Cheaper Edition, with Frontispiece. Crown 8vo, 6s.

TAYLOR, Col. Meadows, C.S.I., M.R.I.A.—**Seeta**: a Novel. New and Cheaper Edition. With Frontispiece. Crown 8vo, 6s.

Tippoo Sultaun: a Tale of the Mysore War. New Edition, with Frontispiece. Crown 8vo, 6s.

Ralph Darnell. New and Cheaper Edition. With Frontispiece. Crown 8vo, 6s.

A Noble Queen. New and Cheaper Edition. With Frontispiece. Crown 8vo, 6s.

The Confessions of a Thug. Crown 8vo, 6s.

Tara: a Mahratta Tale. Crown 8vo, 6s.

Within Sound of the Sea. New and Cheaper Edition, with Frontispiece. Crown 8vo, 6s.

BOOKS FOR THE YOUNG.

Brave Men's Footsteps. A Book of Example and Anecdote for Young People. By the Editor of "Men who have Risen." With 4 Illustrations by C. Doyle. Eighth Edition. Crown 8vo, 3s. 6d.

COXHEAD, Ethel.—**Birds and Babies.** Imp. 16mo. With 33 Illustrations. Cloth gilt, 2s. 6d.

DAVIES, G. Christopher.—**Rambles and Adventures of our School Field Club.** With 4 Illustrations. New and Cheaper Edition. Crown 8vo, 3s. 6d.

EDMONDS, Herbert.—**Well Spent Lives**: a Series of Modern Biographies. New and Cheaper Edition. Crown 8vo, 3s. 6d.

EVANS, Mark.—**The Story of our Father's Love,** told to Children. Fourth and Cheaper Edition of Theology for Children. With 4 Illustrations. Fcap. 8vo, 1s. 6d.

JOHNSON, Virginia W.—**The Catskill Fairies.** Illustrated by Alfred Fredericks. 5s.

MAC KENNA, S. J.—**Plucky Fellows.** A Book for Boys. With 6 Illustrations. Fifth Edition. Crown 8vo, 3s. 6d.

REANEY, Mrs. G. S.—**Waking and Working;** or, From Girlhood to Womanhood. New and Cheaper Edition. With a Frontispiece. Crown 8vo, 3s. 6d.

Blessing and Blessed: a Sketch of Girl Life. New and Cheaper Edition. Crown 8vo, 3s. 6d.

Rose Gurney's Discovery. A Book for Girls. Dedicated to their Mothers. Crown 8vo, 3s. 6d.

English Girls: Their Place and Power. With Preface by the Rev. R. W. Dale. Fourth Edition. Fcap. 8vo, 2s. 6d.

Just Anyone, and other Stories. Three Illustrations. Royal 16mo, 1s. 6d.

Sunbeam Willie, and other Stories. Three Illustrations. Royal 16mo, 1s. 6d.

Sunshine Jenny, and other Stories. Three Illustrations. Royal 16mo, 1s. 6d.

STOCKTON, Frank R.—**A Jolly Fellowship.** With 20 Illustrations. Crown 8vo, 5s.

STORR, Francis, and TURNER, Hawes.—**Canterbury Chimes;** or, Chaucer Tales retold to Children. With 6 Illustrations from the Ellesmere MS. Second Edition. Fcap. 8vo, 3s. 6d.

STRETTON, Hesba.—**David Lloyd's Last Will.** With 4 Illustrations. New Edition. Royal 16mo, 2s. 6d.

Tales from Ariosto Re-told for Children. By a Lady. With 3 Illustrations. Crown 8vo, 4s. 6d.

WHITAKER, Florence.—**Christy's Inheritance.** A London Story. Illustrated. Royal 16mo, 1s. 6d.

PRINTED BY WILLIAM CLOWES AND SONS, LIMITED, LONDON AND BECCLES.

www.ingramcontent.com/pod-product-compliance
Lightning Source LLC
Chambersburg PA
CBHW030608040726
47497CB00008B/2892